Elizabeth Ferrars and The Murder Room

>>> This title is part of The Murder Room, our series dedicated to making available out-of-print or hard-to-find titles by classic crime writers.

Crime fiction has always held up a mirror to society. The Victorians were fascinated by sensational murder and the emerging science of detection; now we are obsessed with the forensic detail of violent death. And no other genre has so captivated and enthralled readers.

Vast troves of classic crime writing have for a long time been unavailable to all but the most dedicated frequenters of second-hand bookshops. The advent of digital publishing means that we are now able to bring you the backlists of a huge range of titles by classic and contemporary crime writers, some of which have been out of print for decades.

From the genteel amateur private eyes of the Golden Age and the femmes fatales of pulp fiction, to the morally ambiguous hard-boiled detectives of mid twentieth-century America and their descendants who walk our twenty-first century streets, The Murder Room has it all. **>>>**

The Murder Room
Where Criminal Minds Meet

themurderroom.com

Elizabeth Ferrars (1907–1995)

One of the most distinguished crime writers of her generation, Elizabeth Ferrars was born Morna Doris MacTaggart in Rangoon and came to Britain at the age of six. She was a pupil at Bedales school between 1918 and 1924, studied journalism at London University and published her first crime novel, *Give a Corpse a Bad Name*, in 1940, the year that she met her second husband, academic Robert Brown. Highly praised by critics, her brand of intelligent, gripping mysteries was also beloved by readers. She wrote over seventy novels and was also published (as E. X. Ferrars) in the States, where she was equally popular. *Ellery Queen Mystery Magazine* described her as 'the writer who may be the closest of all to Christie in style, plotting and general milieu', and the *Washington Post* called her 'a consummate professional in clever plotting, characterization and atmosphere'. She was a founding member of the Crime Writers Association, who, in the early 1980s, gave her a lifetime achievement award.

The Doubly Dead

Elizabeth Ferrars

An Orion book

Copyright © Peter MacTaggart 1963

The right of Elizabeth Ferrars to be identified as the author of this work has
been asserted in accordance with the Copyright, Designs and Patents Act 1988.

This edition published by
The Orion Publishing Group Ltd
Orion House
5 Upper St Martin's Lane
London WC2H 9EA

An Hachette UK company
A CIP catalogue record for this book is available from the British Library

ISBN 978 1 4719 0712 8

www.orionbooks.co.uk

CHAPTER I

ON SATURDAY morning the roof of Margot Dalziel's pretty cottage at the foot of the downs was bright with the glitter of hoar-frost. Rachel Hardwicke, who lived next door, saw the sheen on the thatch when she went into the garden to hang up a drip-dry shirt of her father's. She saw the small rainbows trapped in the whiteness on the silvery grey of the straw and the sharp cold blue of the morning sky and her breath caught at the incredible picture-book charm of it all. At the same time she wondered if there was any point in hanging out the shirt, since it would be as hard as a board in a few minutes.

But the day was unlikely to continue as cold as it had started. The sun was bright and it was rather early in the year for a sustained frost. If the shirt froze up at first, instead of dripping, it would presently thaw out.

The one night of frost, however, had wrought shocking damage among the roses, the only flowers in the garden that had truly survived a summer of neglect while the house had stood empty, and had gone on blooming richly into the autumn. Until yesterday the Queen Elizabeths by the gate had been covered in pink flowers and half-open buds, which to-day had all turned brown and shrivelled.

Rachel knew that that would sadden her father. He had been gloating over those bushes with a sort of tender triumph, as if he had had something to do with producing them himself. In fact, they had been there and blooming away as hard as they could three months ago, when the Hardwickes had first moved in. But Paul Hardwicke was a man who was rather inclined to award himself praise or blame for matters with which he had had very little to do. He was likely now to have an attack of

1

conscience because he had failed to take thought before-hand and somehow protect his roses from the unexpected severity of this November.

Crossing the lawn to where a line for the washing was slung between two trees, Rachel felt the grass crackle stiffly under her feet. As she pegged up the shirt the cold nipped hard at her fingers and her mind jerked suddenly to the danger of frozen pipes. You don't really know a house, she thought, you aren't really at home in it until you know how its pipes behave in a bad winter.

In the small semi-detached house in north London where she and her father had lived for ten years before his retirement, Rachel had had an exasperated but intimate relationship with the plumbing. She had known all the danger-spots and the measures that just might save serious trouble if you were lucky, and which you struggled along with, winter after winter, instead of doing some-thing sensible and efficient about the whole system, because, of course, you weren't staying in the house for ever. As soon as that day of retirement came round, you were moving away to the country.

That had always been her father's daydream. He had liked schoolmastering, but the hope of some day being able to look out of his window at trees and meadows instead of at a row of graceless little houses exactly like his own, had always pulled at his heart. Rachel had never been sure that she wanted the change as much as he did. She had had a job as a physiotherapist in a big London hospital and had been afraid that she might not be able to find anything that promised to be nearly as interesting in another neighbourhood.

And so far, it was true, she had not done so. But she had not yet gone hunting very hard. The move had used up a good deal of her energy and then it had been pleasant for a time to do nothing in particular and then, when she had started to talk of looking for a job, her father had been subtly, if unconsciously, obstructive.

Then, of course, Brian Burden had come into the

picture. For some time now Rachel had found it almost impossible to think wholeheartedly about anything but of when she was likely to see him next. Yet idleness, or rather, being too much at home, for there was never any lack of work to be done about the house and garden, had lately begun to get on her nerves. As she turned now, before going indoors again, to take another look at the sparkling prettiness of the frosted thatch next door, a shadow of moodiness fell across the normal serenity of her face and two little lines, sharper than they should have been at thirty-three, showed between her wide-spaced blue eyes. For a moment she caught herself stupidly envying Margot Dalziel for the life she lived, for her flat in London, her journeys abroad, her wide circle of friends. Stupidly, because Rachel knew that to be assistant editor of a magazine like *Worldwide* and to lead the life that went with it, you had to have both talents and toughness and that she herself entirely lacked the qualities that would make such a life endurable. In her own opinion she was a very ordinary woman, taller and bonier than she would have liked to be, naturally clumsy with her clothes and her make-up, and not even knowing how to make the most of her only good feature, her curly red-gold hair.

When she returned to the house she found her father in the kitchen. He had two main occupations at present. One was painting the bathroom and the other was writing a book on the teaching of biology in schools. That day he had been at work on his book but had interrupted himself to make a mid-morning cup of coffee. Asking Rachel as she came in if she wanted one too while he was at it, he opened the biscuit tin and groped in it for his favourite ginger-nuts.

" I think they're finished," said Rachel, seeing what he was doing. " You had the last ones last night."

" Oh—then I'll have a Digestive." He took three biscuits out of the tin. " What about you? "

" No thank you."

"Not starting to worry about your weight, are you? With your sort of figure, you'll be able to eat all you like all your life and never put on an extra pound."

Paul Hardwicke was very lean himself, a man of medium height with a slight stoop, a quick, shuffling walk, a rosy, lively face and thick white hair. His own appetite for food was hearty and liable to function suddenly at any time of the day, yet his stomach was still as flat as it had been when he was twenty and his knees and his wrists were as bony.

"If you forgot my ginger-nuts when you did the ordering," he said, pouring hot water on to a spoonful of instant coffee, "I could walk down to the shop and get them. I was thinking of seeing if a walk would clear my mind. It looks a nice morning for a walk."

"I was going down to the shop presently myself," said Rachel. "There's a bill to pay."

"Want some money?" he asked.

"No, I've still got some," she said.

"Well, I think I'll go for a walk now anyway," said Paul. "I've got stuck. Stared at a page all the morning and can't make up my mind how to get over the next point I want to make." With a cup in one hand and a biscuit in the other, he leant against the dresser, while Rachel began to scrub some potatoes under the tap. "Of course, it's this reproduction business. In my view it's better not to teach zoology at all in schools than to teach it dishonestly. Yet that's what a lot of schools expect of the teacher. They expect him to get up in front of a class of children whom he's trying to lead into a scientific way of thinking and deliberately lie to them or at best quell their natural, healthy curiosity. . . ."

He was off on one of his hobby-horses, talking swiftly through a mouthful of crumbs.

When he paused for a moment, Rachel said, "Miss Dalziel gets back from Geneva to-day, doesn't she?"

"So she does," he said. "But as I was saying . . ."

He went on saying it, although in the middle of it

Rachel went out to see if she could find enough brussels sprouts for lunch on the plants at the bottom of the garden.

The only difference that finding himself alone made to Paul Hardwicke was that he started to gesture more freely and to declaim more dramatically. But when he had finished his coffee and was munching his last mouthful of biscuit, he wandered out of the kitchen, put on an overcoat and cap, picked up his walking-stick and went out by the front door.

At once he saw what had happened to the roses and stood still, mourning over them.

" I'm really so ignorant," he thought. " I know so very little. I make so many mistakes—like bringing Rachel to live here. And now perhaps it's too late to put that right, because of that fellow Burden. And anyway, I haven't the faintest idea what to do about it."

But it was too cold to stand there sorrowing for more than a moment and as he walked on his thoughts returned to his book and his lips began to move again in animated speech, though no sound came from them.

When he came to Margot Dalziel's gate, he stopped and looked interestedly at the cottage and its big garden. Very cunning about the garden she was, he thought, inducing penniless young men who wanted to write books or paint pictures or some such thing, to come and live rent-free in that old barn of hers down at the end of the orchard and ask in return only that they should keep the place more or less in order. Not that any of them had ever stayed for long, so Paul had heard in the village. Perhaps being relieved of practical cares and finding yourself with nothing to do but write or paint was really a rather horrific experience, or perhaps Miss Dalziel wanted more from them than they had been led to expect.

Young Burden, the barn's present occupant, at least appeared to be taking his duties fairly seriously, for the borders looked reasonably well weeded and most of the dead leaves had been swept up, which was more than Paul had yet done in his own garden. But the dahlias ought to have been lifted before now. The young man had slipped up there. The big bed in front of the cottage had been badly caught by the frost and the flower heads were hanging limply, looking like soggy sponges.

Paul considered going in to see if Miss Dalziel had got home yet. He had had no conscious intention of calling on her when he started his walk, but now it felt as if that had been the purpose that had brought him out. He admired her very much and enjoyed her conversation and felt that it would take his mind off the troublesome problem of his book to hear about the conference in Geneva, from which, as she had told him a week ago, she would be returning to-day. To see her would refresh his mind and stimulate him. And presently he might discuss his problem with her. He could not remember that he had ever heard her express any opinions on education, but a woman of her kind was almost certain to have some, which might well be valuable.

While he hesitated at the gate, the church clock struck. The chimes sounded clear and mellow in the frosty air. It was only eleven o'clock. That was really rather early for Miss Dalziel to have arrived. There would be a better chance of finding her at home if he went for a walk first and called in to see her on his way home again.

Walking on, he passed the entrance to the lane that edged her property and led to her old barn. For most of the year the surface of the lane was a morass of mud and rotting leaves, but to-day, Paul saw, it was frozen hard and its ruts were filled with ice. Three children were rambling along it. Paul knew them by sight. They were part of the Applin brood, who lived in a disgraceful shack at the far end of the lane and were a troublesome lot, although handsome, extraordinarily handsome. The sight of them always troubled him and the fact that they were all so good-looking, with black hair and red cheeks and shining black eyes, when at the same time they were always so much dirtier and raggeder than children usually were these days, somehow made things seem worse.

He waved to the three as he passed, at which they drew together defensively, as if his friendliness were a threat, and began to snigger. Paul sighed. Something ought to be done about them, he had told the vicar, the village schoolmaster and Sergeant Gower. All these had earnestly agreed, had told him just what they themselves had tried to do and said how glad they would be if he would like to try his hand at the problem now.

Education, thought Paul, striding on. You always get back to education.

The eldest of the Applin children, named Kevin, had returned home only a few days ago after doing his first prison sentence for robbing a cigarette-shop in the nearby town of Fallford. He had struck the old woman who owned the shop in the face, breaking her spectacles and cutting one cheek quite badly. Then he had walked out of the shop straight into the arms of a policeman. It had been a brutal and stupid crime, yet the boy looked neither brutal nor stupid. That was what was so disturbing. He looked friendly and quite intelligent and his employer, a market gardener in the neighbourhood, had spoken up for him at his trial, saying that he had been an excellent worker.

Paul lashed irritably with his stick at a stone in the road. It was all so difficult. Everything about education was difficult. One of its worst troubles was that you never had a chance of studying the results of what you had done. You saw the immediate results on the children, but you couldn't keep track of the men whom the children became. You could set up an experiment, but you never saw its conclusion. If there ever was a conclusion. If, in the end, it really made any difference . . .

Paul stood still. His thoughts were taking a direction which they had been taking more and more often of late and which he always found very depressing. It might be best after all to go home, just calling in on Miss

Dalziel on the way, on the chance that she had arrived.

But apparently she had not, for when he reached her cottage and rang the bell, there was no answer. However, as he stood hesitating in the small, rambler-covered porch, a sound from behind the cottage caught his ear, a sound of feet scraping on gravel and of soft whispering voices. Walking round to the back he found the younger two of the three Applin children, whom he had seen in the lane, interestedly watching as the eldest of them, a girl of about twelve, gently tried the door of Miss Dalziel's tool-shed.

She sprang away from it as she heard Paul's footsteps. Giving him a nervous smile, she said rapidly, " Hallo, Mr. Hardwicke—can you tell me the right time, please? "

Automatically Paul looked at his watch and began to answer, " It's a quarter past . . ."

But without waiting for him to finish, the three children had started trotting off to the gate.

" No, no, wait! " Paul shouted after them. " Bernice——" He knew the name of the eldest. " What are you doing here? "

They stood still, Bernice taking up a protective position in front of the other two.

" We came to ask the lady the right time," she said. " Does she keep a clock in that shed? "

Looking down at the ground, Bernice scraped an arc on the gravel with the toe of her shoe. She was wearing a torn red coat, several sizes too small for her. Her thick hair was tied up in a pony tail with a soiled green ribbon. Her cheeks were brilliant with the cold.

" I was calling for the bottles," she said.

" What bottles? "

" The bottles I take back to the Waggoners for her. Sometimes she gives us sixpence."

" Does she keep the bottles in that shed? "

Bernice hesitated for an instant, then said, " Sometimes."

Paul did not believe her any more than he believed that Margot Dalziel paid the children to return her empties to the Waggoners, but he went to the door of the shed and tried it. It was locked.

"There's nothing here for you now, so you'd better push off and don't try this on again, whatever you were really up to," he said.

"No, Mr. Hardwicke," said Bernice submissively. But there was a mocking gleam of satisfaction in her eyes, because she thought that his trying the door of the shed and then telling them to go without threatening them with punishment meant that he had believed her.

The pathetic stupidity of it, Paul thought, the frightening stupidity. If he didn't threaten her, then she had successfully duped him, that was how she had it worked out.

"Well, what are you waiting for?" he asked impatiently, as the three children stood watching him with a furtive sort of contempt behind the blankness of their faces.

"Can you tell us the right time, please?" said Bernice.

"It's a quarter past eleven—but next time go and look at the church clock, and don't come bothering Miss Dàlziel," he said.

"Yes, sir, thank you, sir," they answered in unison.

With Bernice taking a hand of each of the others, they set off down the drive. But they had not even the wit to wait until they were out of sight to go into peals of triumphant giggles.

That depressed Paul almost as much as the lying and the worried feeling that probably, since Margot Dalziel was away so much and the place was left empty so often, he ought to have taken some more energetic action about the children's sneaking round her cottage.

At least he would have to tell her about it when she got back. Then if she wanted him to, he would go and speak to the Applin parents about it. As he started after the children towards the gate, he began to plan what he could say to the parents. He could explain the probable fearful consequences of their neglect, could ask them if they wanted all their children to go the same way as the unspeakable Kevin. Only the trouble about that was that the Applin parents probably wouldn't care in the least if that did happen. They probably thought it an inescapable fate for children of theirs.

And now here was another annoying thing.

Paul had just reached the front of the cottage and noticed that while he had been talking to the children a bottle of milk had been delivered and that the milkman had not troubled to put the old chipped cup, left on the doorstep for the purpose, over the top of the bottle. So now there was a gash in the shiny foil cap where the birds had been at it, drinking the cream.

That triggered off Paul's temper. He knew that Rachel had had a good deal of bother with the man over the same thing, had had to complain again and again because he would not take the very little extra trouble that was needed to deal with the birds. Reaching home and telling her fumingly about the bottle on Miss Dalziel's doorstep, he demanded that Rachel should tell him that this was but another sign of a general lowering of standards.

Rachel was sitting by the window in the living-room, stitching up a torn seam in one of the old skirts that she wore about the house and garden.

" We've got some spare milk to-day," she said. " I can take a bottle round to Miss Dalziel presently when I go to the shop."

" Ah, good," said Paul. " Yes, do. And if you see her, you might mention that I found the Applin children prowling round her toolshed and sent them off." He scratched his head and frowned. " I feel I ought probably to have done something a bit more drastic, but I'm damned if I know what. I hope they hadn't actually pinched anything before I got there."

" They may not have been going to pinch anything," said Rachel. " I've often caught them prowling around the garden, but I haven't missed anything yet except a few apples and those may have been taken by any of the village children. I think it's mainly curiosity and having nothing else to do."

" That may be all it is at present, but what will it be in two or three years' time? " said Paul. " Bernice is a practised liar already."

" But she's got some good qualities, haven't you noticed? " said Rachel. " Look at the way she looks after the younger ones."

" Because they're her gang and she's the leader."

" Not just because she's really naturally good-hearted? "

" Oh, my dear, she may be as naturally good-hearted as an angel, but without either a decent home or reasonable intelligence, what hope is there for her? Well, I'd better get back to work."

Paul wandered out, feeling that perhaps the best way to escape his uncomfortable thoughts about the Applin children was to return to the problem of how to instruct children from nice, sympathetic homes in the first principles of biology, for that, after all, was a highly important thing to do, if they were to grow up good, well-adjusted citizens of the modern world.

Rachel finished her mending, then put on her tweed coat, fetched a bottle of milk from the refrigerator and her bicycle from the garage and set off for Miss Dalziel's cottage and the village.

She did not after all leave the milk on Miss Dalziel's doorstep. When she got there, she found that the bottle with the punctured cap had gone, and that meant, she supposed, that Miss Dalziel had arrived on the eleven-forty-five, the train on which she most often travelled when she came down to her cottage for the week-end, and had taken in her milk.

It might perhaps have been neighbourly to ring and offer her a bottle of milk that had not been sampled by the birds, but Rachel did not want to risk being asked to come in, pressed to drink some sherry and delayed until after the village shop had shut for the lunch hour. She always found Miss Dalziel rather overpowering and had not yet acquired the knack of refusing her invitations in a friendly but firm fashion. Hoping that she had not been seen from the cottage, Rachel returned to her bicycle, put the bottle of milk back into the basket on her handlebars and rode on to the village.

She felt slightly guilty at hurrying off in that way, but she was quite without any suspicion that she would later regret it more than anything that she had ever done in her life.

CHAPTER II

IN THE village shop Rachel met Mrs. Godfrey, secretary of the Women's Institute, who startled her by suggesting that she should give a talk to the women of the village on her work in the hospital. The invitation filled Rachel with a mixture of pleasure and pure panic. She had never spoken in public in her life and could not really imagine herself ever doing so and she said so without giving herself time to think. Mrs. Godfrey, an energetic, tweedy little widow whom Rachel suspected of having cast an interested eye on her father smilingly accepted the refusal, but there was a look in her calm grey eyes which warned Rachel that she had not heard the end of the matter. In her confusion she got through her shopping as fast as she could, leapt on to her bicycle and rode off home again. It was not until half-way through the afternoon that she realised that she had forgotten the ginger-nuts for her father.

When this happened she was in the garden, raking up the dead leaves scattered over the lawn. There had been a thaw and there was a pleasant earthy scent in the air and a stillness that felt like the last gentle leave-taking of the autumn. She was enjoying it and did not want to interrupt herself to go back to the village. The biscuits, she decided, could wait until it had grown too dark for her to go on working in the garden. So it was not until half past five and dusk was falling that she got on to her bicycle again and rode back to the shop.

In passing Miss Dalziel's cottage this time, Rachel noticed that there was a black car in the drive. She also saw the figure of a man outlined against the light-coloured paint of the cottage door. She saw that the car did not belong to Roderick Dalziel, a nephew of Miss Dalziel who often visited her, but was something a good deal larger and more opulent than his, and she saw that the man himself was not Roderick. Apart from that, Rachel did not notice anything much about either man or car. She went to the shop, bought the ginger-nuts and returned homewards, the whole errand taking about ten minutes.

By then darkness was falling fast and when she passed the cottage again its garden was in deep shadow, so she did not see the man, although he was standing in the gateway. She only saw him when she got off her bicycle at her own gate, and turning, because she heard quick footsteps on the road behind her, found herself face to face with him.

He was tall and slender and was wearing a dark over-coat. In the near-darkness she could not tell his age, but she thought that his hair was grey. His voice, when he spoke, was pleasant but hurried and rather nervous.

" I'm sorry to trouble you," he said, " but I wonder if you can tell me if my sister's come home. She's supposed to be expecting me, but she doesn't seem to be in."

" Do you mean Miss Dalziel? " asked Rachel.

" Yes—I'm sorry, I should have explained," he said. " I'm Neil Dalziel, her brother. I've hung around for almost half an hour, in case she'd had to go out for some reason, but there's still no sign of her, so I've begun to wonder if she's come home at all."

" I think she has," said Rachel. " I haven't actually seen her, but I think she came home this morning on her usual train. Are you sure she's expecting you? "

13

" Oh yes," he said. " She rang me up yesterday evening and asked me to come down. She said it was urgent."

" Then perhaps she's had to go to the village for something," said Rachel. " Only I've just been to the shop myself and she wasn't there."

She hesitated, wondering where else Miss Dalziel might have gone for what had been intended only as a quick visit, but which had somehow been prolonged.

" There's the barn, of course," she said.

" The barn! " the man said promptly. " That must be it. It's because of something to do with the barn that she wanted me to come down all of a sudden. All the same, how she thought I was to guess . . . But still, I ought to have thought of it without bothering you. Thank you so much for your help. I'm sure you're right. Thank you."

He turned to go.

" Wait a moment," Rachel said. " Do you know where it is? "

" I don't think I actually do," he said, " but I expect I can find it."

" You go past her gate to the first turning beyond it," said Rachel. " There's a lane there. It's rather muddy, I'm afraid. And the barn's on the left. It's the first building you come to. If you like I could——"

" Thank you," he said again, interrupting her just as she was about to suggest that she should show him the way, since the lane was dark as well as muddy and it would be a simple matter for her to light it up for him with her bicycle lamp. " Thank you, that's very clear. I'll find it easily. You've been very kind. Good night."

He was in such a hurry to be gone that Rachel did not try again to help him.

As he walked off rapidly into the darkness, she wheeled her bicycle through the gate, put it away in the garage and let herself into the house. Inside, she heard voices and for a moment she stood still, wondering whether or

not to go after the stranger and tell him that she had sent
him on a fool's errand, because Brian Burden was here.
When Neil Dalziel had floundered along the dark, muddy
lane, he would find the barn as deserted as he had found
the cottage, unless, of course, Miss Dalziel sometimes
visited the barn when Brian was out. Perhaps, Rachel
thought, Brian would know if she ever did that. On the
whole it seemed reasonable to ask him about that before
dashing off after the other man.

Apart from what was reasonable, Brian's voice always
acted on Rachel like a magnet. At any time the unexpected
sound of it, or sometimes even a stray thought of him,
brought a tightness to her throat and started her heart
thudding. He was by far the most important thing just
then in her existence.

She thought that he probably knew this. But it was
hard to be sure. Brian's big, impassive, ruddy face really
gave very little away. To begin with, Rachel had mistaken it for stupid, and had thought that if Margot
Dalziel seriously expected this large, slow-thinking, slow-
spoken young man to produce a book of any interest, she
must be more naïve than she appeared. If, on the other
hand, she did not seriously expect it, but had merely
recognised that after his fashion Brian would be con-
scientious about looking after her garden, whether he ever
got a book written or not, then she must be a much more
calculating person than she appeared, perhaps even a
rather horrid person.

However, after knowing Brian for several weeks, Rachel
had decided that all that Miss Dalziel need have been
was perceptive, for behind Brian's hesitancy, his apparently
bewildered silences, his unwillingness to commit himself
to any but the fuzziest of opinions, Rachel had come to
believe that there was an unusually observant and
penetrating mind. His slowness, she had come to think,
was the result of his having a little too much to cope with
all at once going on inside him, a sort of rich confusion
of ideas and impressions, which he felt that he had to

arrange for himself before it could make sense to anyone else.

For instance, when his short-sighted stare settled on her face, Rachel always felt that he knew at once what happened in her when she saw him, that she had been seen through without any difficulty, and that the state of her feelings was being filed away for interested consideration later.

As she came into the room now, Brian got to his feet but characteristically said nothing, simply standing there, smiling at her and waiting passively for whatever might happen next.

He had a heavy, loose-jointed body, long arms and big, rough hands. Their palms were broad, and the fingers were short and square-tipped. With fingers like that, thought Rachel, it was one of the odd things about him that his hand-writing should be remarkably small and neat.

Coming forward to the fire, she said, " Someone who says he's Miss Dalziel's brother has just been asking me if I've seen her. He'd been to the cottage, he said, and she wasn't there. I said I thought she got home this morning, but I hadn't seen her. Have you seen her, Brian? "

" No, not to-day," he said.

" I sent him along to the barn, in case she'd gone there to see you," she said. " He said he was expected and he seemed to be in a hurry."

Her father said, " Her brother—that means he's Roderick's father, I suppose. I don't know why, but I've always taken for granted Roderick hadn't any parents."

" He hasn't," said Brian. He had remained standing, seeming to need some time to make up his mind whether to sit down again, or to go out after the stranger. To Rachel, who had sat down in a low chair by the fire, he appeared to take up a great deal of space in the small room, to fill it with his breadth and his warmth, almost in the way that the thought of him filled her mind.

" There's another brother," he said. " I've never met him. I don't think he and Margot see much of each other."

" He said she'd asked him down because of something to do with the barn," said Rachel.

Brian looked blank. " I don't know anything about that," he said.

" Do you think she might be there now? " she asked.

" No, I don't think so."

" Do sit down, Brian," Paul Hardwicke said irritably. Brian's big shadow was making it difficult for him to see to fill his pipe. " You'll probably miss him if you go after him. Sit down."

" I was just wondering why . . ." Brian paused, then suddenly reached the point of decision and sat down. " I think he's an architect," he said. " Yes, I think that's it."

" Then perhaps she's going to dress the place up a bit and sell it," said Paul.

" The barn? " said Rachel, with a sudden sensation of cold at her heart.

Brian gave Paul a thoughtful look. " Yes," he said slowly. " Of course it could easily be turned into a good week-ending sort of place that would sell for quite a lot of money. Seal up some of the cracks where the wind gets in and put in a bathroom—that's all you'd have to do. It's picturesque as hell as it is, isn't it? "

" And an easy distance from London," said Paul, nodding. " And she could get rid of some of her ground with it, which is really too much for her at present, and there's no risk of building near it, that I know of, or of that lane being turned into a sixty-foot by-pass to any-where."

" Yes," said Brian, frowning down at the fire, " I shouldn't be at all surprised if you're right. It's never occurred to me, but that barn must be quite a valuable property."

" Worth three or four thousand anyway," said Paul,

and looked unreasonably satisfied with his business acumen.

To Rachel it seemed that it meant nothing to him that if the barn were sold, Brian would return to some such dreary London bed-sitting-room as he had probably come from and at once, in his hesitating, undeliberate way, fade out of her life.

But perhaps he had already been planning to go back to London. Perhaps the book had not made as good progress as he had hoped, or perhaps it was finished. Rachel knew very little about the book because she had realised that it embarrassed Brian profoundly to be questioned about it.

" I never thought of Miss Dalziel *needing* money," she said.

For once Brian answered quickly. " Everyone needs money."

" But has she ever talked about this to you? " she asked.

" No," he said.

" Then it's just one of Daddy's ideas. He may be quite wrong."

" Yes, but . . ." Brian paused and Rachel had the feeling that he had started to think about something quite different. " I *think* her brother's an architect," he said after a little. " But I could be wrong about that. Perhaps she said an accountant. Or an agriculturalist. Or an acrobat. I rather hope so."

" Even if he's an architect," said Rachel, " she may just be thinking of putting a bathroom in for you."

Brian gave an abstracted smile. " Perhaps. It seems to me I'm turning into such a good gardener, I deserve one."

" Doesn't she let you use the bath in the cottage? " Paul asked " You've got a key, haven't you? "

" Well, yes," said Brian, " but I'm scared of the place."

" Scared? " said Rachel, puzzled. " What is it, a ghost, or a geyser that blows up, or something? "

18

" No, but her standards of tidiness are so frightfully high," said Brian, " and that brings out the wild animal in me. Whenever I go in I feel sure I'm going to smash something precious to bits with my damned great hooves."

Rachel laughed and stood up. " I shouldn't worry about it, anyhow. She wouldn't suddenly turn you out without warning. I'd better start doing something about supper now. Are you staying, Brian? "

That was the sort of question that he had to turn over carefully in his mind before he answered. While he considered it, his eyes remained on her face and the tension in Rachel began to mount.

" Would it be an awful nuisance if I did? " he asked at last.

" Of course not," she said.

" It's awfully good of you."

" I'm afraid it's only eggs."

" Can I come and help then? Eggs are things I know about." He smiled at her and Rachel smiled back far more radiantly than she knew. She suggested that he might come and make the toast.

To her surprise, her father said sharply that making the toast was his job, that he always made the toast, that he had a particular way of making toast and that no other would do. Not a word of it was true. He added that what Brian ought to do, if he was staying, was to sit by the fire with a drink and the evening paper.

As if he had not heard any of it, Brian got to his feet and followed Rachel to the kitchen.

Behind them the evening paper suddenly crackled noisily. A cupboard door slammed and a bottle and glass jarred loudly together as Paul got a drink for himself. Although he knew all about Rachel's feeling for Brian, he had been taken by surprise by that sudden glow of happiness on her face. He would have to start taking care, he thought, as he somehow restrained himself from giving the fire a vicious poking. He did not want Rachel to come to the conclusion that he was a jealous old man, determined to keep her for himself. For that wasn't the trouble at all. He thought that she ought to marry, wished that it would happen soon, worried that she might let her love for him become a burdensome obligation, or even an excuse for not venturing out into rougher waters. But that young man was no good.

Paul believed that Brian was the kind of man who would never stick to anything, would never make a home for her, would expect her to lead him by the hand through life and probably not even be faithful to her. She didn't realise that, of course. She probably didn't even realise that in spite of his slowness and quietness, Brian was charged with a vitality that would have the same effect on almost every woman he met as he had had on her and that he would always enjoy this and exploit it.

And it had been Paul's determination to leave London that had made her particularly vulnerable, since it had turned out that Brian was the only man under fifty for miles around.

Paul found that a horribly depressing thought. It had been depressing him seriously, on and off, for the last month, because he found it extremely distressing to think of himself as inconsiderate where Rachel was concerned. Trying to make up for it, he did his best to appear to be back in his usual good temper when she and Brian returned from the kitchen with supper on the trolley. They ate it sitting round the fire, and when Brian left at about ten o'clock, Paul saw him to the gate, then walked a little way home with him, saying that the fresh air would make him sleep better.

The night felt very cold. The ground had hardened again and the sky was ablaze with frostily brilliant stars. Paul walked with Brian as far as the beginning of the lane that led to the barn, then turned back. He had had an idea, when he started out that he might drop in on Miss Dalziel for a few minutes, just to ask if she had found everything in order and to mention his encounter with the

Applin children and Rachel's with Miss Dalziel's brother.
And then, he had thought, while he was at it, perhaps he
might ask her what her intentions were about the barn,
because if by any chance she was really going to sell it,
that would probably solve the problem of Brian.

But there were no lights in the cottage. Apparently
Miss Dalziel had gone to bed early. Abandoning the idea
of calling on her, Paul hurried home to the fire.

CHAPTER III

NEXT MORNING there was a haziness in the air that
threatened fog and the roads were treacherous with ice.
Rachel and her father went to church, walking fast to
warm themselves though, keeping a wary eye on the
frozen puddles. After the service they gratefully accepted
a lift home from Mrs. Godfrey, asking her in for a drink,
when they got there. She hesitated, doubted if she had the
time, then thought that she would come in for just two
minutes.

Rachel left her in the care of her father and went to the
tool shed, fetched the secateurs and started snipping off
the frost-bitten blooms from the rose bushes by the gate,
the sight of which offended her this morning. The weather
offended her too. Yesterday she had enjoyed it, but
to-day the frost seemed to have touched her bones,
shrivelling up something inside her. She felt irritable and
depressed and prepared to lose her temper with somebody.

This was a state of mind to which she was not much
accustomed, although she had suffered from it rather
more than usual during the last few weeks. Unsure of
where it came from, she connected the particular mood
of to-day with her father's attitude to Brian. She had
never realised until the evening before that he did not

21

like Brian. He liked most people, at least if they showed any signs of liking him, which Brian had plainly done from the first. Yet last night Paul's face had been twitching with antagonism.

Maliciously, while she snipped off dead rose-buds, Rachel wondered how he was coping with Mrs. Godfrey, who had already out-stayed her two minutes and who was immensely strong-minded in her quiet way. She had the good-natured serenity of a woman who is fairly confident of getting most of what she wants and who has the habit of gently and unthinkingly steam-rollering all resistance flat. However, if there was any woman in the neighbourhood by whom Paul had shown signs of being impressed, it was Margot Dalziel. Her sophistication awed him while her warm friendliness charmed him. As long as she went on spending her week-ends in the cottage next door, Rachel did not think that the little widow would ever get very far with him.

A screech of tyres, skidding on the icy road, startled her. She looked up sharply. A car had just stopped opposite the gate. But it looked as if this had happened merely by chance, for the man and the woman inside the car were showing no interest in the house or in Rachel, but were locked in each other's arms and passionately kissing.

Rachel turned to go indoors, leaving them at it, when she heard her name called.

" Oh, hallo, Rachel! "

She turned back and saw that the man, who was releasing the girl and who now smiled cheerfully at Rachel, was Margot Dalziel's nephew, Roderick.

" Cold morning, isn't it? " he went on. " This is my wife."

Rachel looked rather blank. When she had last seen Roderick he had not been married, or even near it, so far as she knew.

" I mean it, you know," he said. " She married me last week. Her name's Jane. And this is Rachel, Jane—

one of our neighbours, if we're going to live in the barn. Rachel Hardwicke."

Rachel felt something strange happen to her face when he mentioned the barn. She tried to control it, but knew that she did not succeed. She managed to force a smile, however.

" So that explains the Mystery of the Red Barn," she said. She went out into the road and stood beside the car. " We knew something was happening, but our guesses have been quite wide of the mark."

" Haven't you seen Margot, then? " Roderick asked.

" Not this week-end," said Rachel.

" She's here, though, isn't she? " he said.

" Of course she's here," said Jane. She had a light, soft voice, and she looked to Rachel incredibly young, although she had a feeling that that was more because of something in Jane's expression than because of her actual years. She was wrapped up in a sheepskin jacket, which hid most of her as she sat in the car, but she gave the impression of being small and very thin. Her skin had a fine transparency and her fair hair, cut in feathery little wisps all over her head, had the softness of down. " She's expecting us," Jane added.

" Yes," said Roderick, " but if something had come up in London . . ."

" She'd have rung up Mummy and told us," said Jane.

" Yes, I suppose so."

But a shadow passed over Roderick's face as he said it, and it occurred to Rachel that he might have been relieved if she had told him that his aunt was not here.

He was remarkably like her in appearance, not so very much the taller of the two, slenderly and gracefully built, as she was, brown haired and dark eyed, with a pointed face and delicate features. It was a face of vivid and quick changes, but on the whole more sombre than his aunt's, although he was only twenty-five and she was at least forty.

" Well, we ought to be getting on," he said. " We're pretty late already."

But instead of driving on, he started to get out of the car. There was an absent-minded frown on his face and Rachel wondered if he could have forgotten for the moment that they had not yet reached Miss Dalziel's cottage, but were still fifty yards or so from her gate. Still with that absent air, he opened the near-door of the car and hauled out two suitcases.

" Darling——" Jane began to protest.

" Wait here a moment," he muttered. " I'll just go and see. . . ." And he went striding off down the road with the cases to Miss Dalziel's gate.

Jane gave a helpless little laugh.

" Isn't he utterly absurd? " she said with tremendous pride in her voice, as if Roderick's absurdities were an important part of his charm for her. " He's terrified of Margot, you know. I can't think of anything funnier. He thinks she'd bite our heads off now for being a tiny bit late and he's gone ahead to get it over—I suppose because, if she did, he'd feel awfully humiliated in front of me. But she won't, of course. She's about the sweetest person I've ever met."

" A bit formidable, though," said Rachel. " She frightens me."

Jane looked at her in amazement. " I adore her," she said. " I'm ever so much fonder of her than I am of my own family. We've just come from visiting them and the strain of it has practically worn me out, though actually Roderick was wonderful with them. But I'm going to love living at the barn. You know, it was one of the first things Margot thought of when Roderick told her we'd got married. That was on Friday evening. We got married suddenly while she was away in Geneva and he was expecting her to be furious—that was partly because he hadn't realised how well she and I get on and that she's really always rather wished we'd get married—well, so of course she wasn't furious at all, but said we could have the barn. . . ."

She paused, eyeing Rachel with intent curiosity.

Rachel knew that this was because her cheeks had started to burn and because she could not control her frown. Last night she had told Brian that he had no need to worry about being turned out of the barn because Miss Dalziel would never do such a thing without warning him. Apparently she had been wrong.

Wondering if this girl knew that the barn already had an occupant, she said, " I suppose she's going to put in a bathroom for you."

" Oh yes, and a nice kitchen," said Jane happily, " and do something about the roof. She rang up her brother straight away—he's an architect—and arranged for his to come down for the week-end, so that we could all discuss it."

" Yes," Rachel said. " I met him yesterday."

" Oh, then I suppose he told you about Roderick and me getting married," said Jane.

" No," said Rachel, " he only said he'd come down to see Miss Dalziel but that she didn't seem to be there—" She stopped because Roderick had just reappeared at the gate of the cottage and had started towards them. He was almost running and his face was oddly distracted.

" Oh, don't say they've quarrelled after all! " Jane exclaimed. " I couldn't bear that. Not to-day. To-day's got to be a wonderful day."

Roderick stood still facing Rachel and spoke to her, not to Jane. His voice was higher than usual.

" I'm afraid it looks as if something's wrong in there," he said. " It's queer. I don't understand it. It looks— rather horrible. But I don't know . . . Perhaps I'm imagining things. Would you come in with us, Rachel, and tell me what you think? If you don't mind. I'd be immensely grateful."

He turned and at once started back to the cottage.

Rachel hurried after him. " Isn't she there, then? " she asked.

" Not now," said Roderick.

" But she has been, hasn't she? "

" It looks like it."

" I think she came yesterday morning."

" Yes. Perhaps. You'll see."

Roderick spoke with a queer tightness of the throat. As they reached the cottage, he went ahead of Rachel, pushed open the door, went straight across the tiny, low-ceilinged hall and down the two steps into the sitting-room.

Nearly falling over the two suitcases which Roderick had left at the bottom of the steep, narrow staircase, Rachel followed him.

The cottage was warm, the warmth coming from the electric central heating which was left on from one end of the winter to the other, whether Miss Dalziel was there or not. Besides this, at some time a fire had been lit in the great open fireplace in the sitting-room. Now, however, there was only a heap of ashes on the hearth, so the fire might have been out for hours or for days, there was no telling which. Rachel vaguely took in that fact, feeling that there was something puzzling about it, something not in order, while she was trying to make sense of the apparently far stranger things in the charming little room.

They added up to something that scared her as they had scared Roderick. Near the fireplace a low coffee-table lay on its side and a decanter of sherry had been dropped on to the edge of the brick hearth and broken. The sherry had made a sticky-looking stain on the hearth-rug, which was awry and in wrinkles. An upright wooden chair was on its back. One sherry-glass had somehow rolled away several feet without breaking and a woman's hand-bag lay on a rug in the middle of the room, with its contents tumbled out in a heap.

There was also a scent of roses in the room. There were some yellow roses in a glass vase on a little writing-table at one side of the window. They were past their first freshness, but still spread their sweetness over the disturbing scene.

" Well? " Roderick asked, looking intently, anxiously at Rachel.

" I don't know," she said. " Is she—have you looked upstairs? "

" I just rushed up and down again," said Roderick. " Her things are there—I mean, her fur coat's on the bed and there's a suitcase. It's open. . . ." He looked muddled for a moment. " It's open. Yes, but, I don't think it's been unpacked—just had a few things pulled out of it. But I'm not sure. I only took a glance at it. Perhaps we'd better go up and see."

Jane had slipped quietly into the room past Rachel and had gone to Roderick. She was standing beside him, holding on to his hand and looking round. Rachel thought that they looked like a pair of children, far too young to have to cope with disaster and holding tight to each other to defend themselves against the inexplicable horrors of the adult world.

It made her feel as if she represented that world and must put her knowledge of it and her greater maturity at their disposal. She would have to go upstairs and all round the rest of the cottage. She would have to think out the meaning of the scene in this room and what they would have to do about it.

" Look at that! " said Jane softly. She pointed with a childish sort of forthrightness at a stain on the rug in the middle of the room. " It's blood, isn't it? "

Jane had very large, dark blue eyes and they looked even more enormous than usual in a face that had lost all its colour. Her heavy sheepskin coat had fallen open showing how little covering she had on her bones. Her hands were like little, delicate, white claws. Her feet were so narrow that there was something astonishing

27

about the fact that they could support a human weight.

" Of course it isn't blood," said Roderick sharply. " It's—mud, or something."

" It's blood! " said Jane. Her voice had gone higher. " I can't stand the sight of blood. Whatever are we going to *do*, darling? "

" First, take another look round," said Rachel.

She turned to the door and Roderick started to follow her. But Jane stood rigidly where she was, staring blindly at the thing that she could not bear to look at, as if hypnotised by it.

At the foot of the stairs, Roderick said in Rachel's ear, " Rachel, do you think you could get Jane away from here as soon as we've looked round? I don't know what's happened, but she's got a terrific imagination. She'll make the very worst of everything."

" All right, I'll take her home, if she'll come with me," said Rachel. " She might prefer to stay with you."

They went up the stairs, bobbing their heads to dodge the low beam half-way up.

" I'd sooner get her away," said Roderick. " She's given to nightmares. Is your father at home now? "

" Yes. I'll ask him to come round, if you like."

" Oh, would you? He'd probably know what we ought to do about—well, the police, perhaps—if things here look the same to him as they do to me."

" Perhaps we're only having nightmares ourselves," said Rachel. " There may be some quite ordinary explanation."

But she could not think of one. There had been a fight in that room downstairs. And blood had been spilt. And Margot Dalziel was missing.

Her bedroom was small, with a sloping ceiling and two small windows with leaded panes. One was slightly open. There was a three-quarter-length ocelot coat lying on the glazed cotton counterpane on the bed. On the floor near the bed was a black glove. It looked as if the coat and gloves had been hastily thrown down and that the glove had slipped down unnoticed to the floor. There was a fibre-glass suitcase on a chair. Its lid was up and one corner of its neatly packed contents had been disturbed, as if something had been hurriedly pulled out from under the carefully folded clothes. On the dressing-table, which consisted of a low mahogany chest-of-drawers with an old oval looking-glass standing on it, a porcelain powder-bowl had had its lid removed and there was a smudge of powder across the polished top of the chest.

Taking these things in one by one, Rachel found herself looking at the closed doors of a built-in hanging cupboard in a corner of the room. She said, " Ought we, do you think. . . ? "

Roderick went to the cupboard and opened it. There was nothing inside but a row of dresses on hangers.

Closing the cupboard again, he said, " Actually I'm sure she isn't in the cottage. But come on—let's look round the rest of it. Then there's the garden. We ought to look everywhere."

He led Rachel into the only other bedroom, in which the twin beds had not been made up, but had blankets folded in piles on the bare mattresses, and which showed no signs of having been entered since it was last cleaned. Then they went into the bathroom where they saw that a towel on the hot rail was crumpled, that there were some dried smears of soap around the almost new tablet in the soap-dish of the hand-basin, and that someone had put down a plastic toilet-case with its zipper undone on the cork-seated chair.

" What it looks like," said Rachel thoughtfully, " is as if Miss Dalziel came up here in a great hurry, dumped her coat and gloves on the bed, got her washing-things out of her suitcase, had a quick wash, dabbed on some powder, then went downstairs and got out the sherry."

" She must have been in a hurry because she was expecting someone," Roderick interrupted. " There are those roses, too. . . ."

" She had time to arrange them, though," said Rachel. " And she took in the milk."

" The milk? " he asked.

Rachel explained. " My father came round yesterday morning to see if she'd got home and he saw the milk bottle on the doorstep with a hole pecked in the top by the birds, so presently I came round with another bottle for her, but I found she'd already taken it in."

" Didn't you see her, then? "

" No, I was in rather a hurry to get to the shop before they shut for the lunch-hour, so I went straight on." Rachel felt a sudden chill in her bones. " If I hadn't, if I'd stayed, if she'd had someone else here with her . . ."

" You couldn't have known," said Roderick brusquely. " Now let's look round outside."

He went to the head of the staircase. Jane was at the bottom of it, looking up at them with the same blind stare in her great eyes.

" Has something awful happened? " she asked. " Is it murder? "

That was when it occurred to Rachel that frightened as the girl might be of the sight of blood, she was not afraid to use a word which Rachel herself could not have brought out at that moment for anything in the world.

Roderick ran down the stairs, put an arm round Jane and drew her to the front door.

" We're going round to the Hardwickes' house," he said, " and Rachel's going to ask her father to come back with me and see what he thinks we ought to do. I think perhaps we ought to call the police, and I expect Mr. Hardwicke knows much more about that sort of thing than we do."

He kept Jane moving on to the gate.

Following them, Rachel wondered on what he had based his estimate of her father. It would never have occurred to her to think of him as knowledgeable about police matters. But perhaps it was merely that Roderick turned automatically to an older person when trouble loomed ahead. Or it might be that his apparent desire for her father's company was only a manœuvre to get Jane away from the cottage.

There was something touching about that, Rachel thought, as she walked behind the two close-linked figures. She would not have thought that Roderick had it in him. It was true that she did not know him at all well, but she had taken for granted till now that he had not much warmth of heart or interest in anyone but himself. That might have been, she supposed, because she had seldom seen him except in the company of his aunt. There had always been something curiously cold and wary in his response to her, as if he were half-afraid of her obvious affection for him, and constantly ready to resist its demands.

They found Paul Hardwicke alone. Mrs. Godfrey had gone and Paul was waiting impatiently for lunch, solacing himself in the meantime with a few biscuits. He had been upstairs when Jane and Roderick had first arrived and had watched their meeting with Rachel from the window of his study. He had seen Roderick go off to the cottage and return, and had realised that there was a certain excitement in the air, but he had not thought of it as boding trouble. Now, when Rachel began to tell him about the situation in the cottage, he maintained an air of abstraction which she knew was intended to convey to her that all his thoughts were on lunch and that he thought that they should be sitting down to it immediately.

But when he realised that this interruption in the normal Sunday programme was not merely social, that something serious appeared to have happened, he said, "Yes, of course I'll come—at once, at once." He looked round for his coat, which was hanging on a peg just in front of him. "Rachel, take Mrs. Dalziel in and give her a cup of tea. And don't start worrying. Please don't worry. I'm sure it's not necessary."

He gave Jane his kindest, most reassuring smile.

Thinking that she looked like a scared bird that had somehow got trapped in a room and was preparing to batter itself to exhaustion against the mysterious invisible menace of the windows, he started off to the cottage with Roderick.

CHAPTER IV

STEERING JANE into the living-room, Rachel said, " Would you like some tea, or would you really like a drink better? I think there's some whisky."

" Some whisky would be wonderful," said Jane. She dropped into a chair with a sigh and closed her eyes.

Rachel went to the cupboard where the drinks were kept. " Water or soda? "

" Just by itself, please."

Rachel poured some whisky into a glass and brought it to Jane, gave her a cigarette and lit one for herself, then sat down on the arm of a chair, watching as the frail-looking creature swallowed the whisky.

" I suppose," said Jane after a moment, " something horrible must have happened. You think so, don't you? "

Rachel tried to make herself say that she did not, found that she could not and did not answer.

" Yes," said Jane. " But I don't see how it could have had anything to do with Roderick and me getting married, do you? "

" Of course not," said Rachel.

" I've been thinking, you see," said Jane. " I've been thinking about Margot and Roderick. They've such a very complicated sort of relationship, so I started to wonder . . ." She gave Rachel a sad look of apology. " I'm dreadfully stupid, I'm afraid. Everyone says so."

Bewildered, Rachel said, " You don't mean to say

you're afraid Roderick came over here and—and did any of that!"

"Oh no!" said Jane, looking astonished. "That never even crossed my mind. Darling Roderick. He couldn't hurt a fly. Besides, he adores Margot."

"What did you mean, then?" Rachel asked.

Jane looked down at her glass, hiding the blank, scared look in her eyes.

"Nothing at all, really," she said. "I'm in a muddle, that's all."

"Are you afraid Miss Dalziel perhaps wasn't as pleased about your marriage as she seemed? Though even if she wasn't, I don't see how that could have had anything to do with whatever happened in the cottage."

"No," said Jane in a low voice. "I can't either."

"I believe you're just a bit afraid she wasn't really pleased," said Rachel.

Jane looked up quickly. "No, I'm not—not at all. It's really Roderick I've been puzzling about. For some reason he was so awfully sure Margot would be furious about our getting married, although I kept telling him she and I were wonderful friends. So I've been wondering if perhaps he really wanted her to be furious and that's why he insisted on our getting married without letting her know. Do you think that's possible?"

"To spite her, for some reason, do you mean?"

"No, no, no, just the other way round! To convince himself she really loved him so much she could hardly bear to part with him."

"I don't know," said Rachel, beginning to feel out of her depth. "I don't know much about that sort of thing."

"She means an awful lot to him, you see," said Jane. "His father was killed in Malaya in the war and though his mother got home safely with Roderick, she got pneumonia only a little while afterwards and died and so Margot brought Roderick up. And his parents hadn't any money to leave, so he's always been quite dependent on her and sometimes he seems to get queer attacks of hating her for it, although really he adores her." She drank up the last drops of her whisky and with great pride in her voice, added, " He's an extraordinarily complicated person."

Rachel said nothing, wondering if this queer girl could really be afraid that her husband had made away with his aunt because she had not been as annoyed by his marriage as he had hoped.

After a moment Jane went on, " Once we'd got married, he was so afraid of what Margot would say about it that he wanted us to go away and not let her know anything about it. I had to insist on his going to meet her at the airport on Friday and telling her straight away—because I didn't think anything else would be right. And then she told him it was what she's been wanting for ages and almost straight away she offered him that old barn of hers for us to live in, and she rang up her brother and asked him to come down here to meet us and talk over just what we'd like done. And she even said something about her will. . . ." Jane suddenly shut her eyes again as if against some ugly vision. " No, I can't talk about that now. At the time it only seemed a nice sort of gesture that of course didn't mean anything, but if something's happened to her . . ."

" Oh, I see," said Rachel vaguely, because her thoughts had not followed Jane beyond her remarks about the barn.

Getting up, she went to the fireplace and threw the remains of her cigarette into the fire. She felt a strange sort of relief that the question of the barn was settled, that Brian's departure was certain. It would have come sooner or later. She had always known that one day, probably without warning, the barn would be empty and Brian quietly gone.

All the same, she thought, what a mean trick to play on him!

" What will Roderick do when he's living here—I mean, for a job? " she asked.

" Oh, we've been having all sorts of ideas," said Jane.
" He hasn't any job at all at present, so that's no difficulty.
And I expect Margot has some ideas too. He's done all
sorts of different things already, you know. He's wonderfully adaptable."

The doorbell rang and Rachel, glad to be interrupted
before she showed too obviously how her blood boiled
when she thought of the old barn with a new kitchen and
new bathroom and new bright curtains and of course a
lot of trailing green plants in pots, and a young married
couple living there, went to answer it.

It was the back-door bell that had rung. Going to the
kitchen and opening the door, Rachel found Bernice
Applin standing there. At first Rachel thought that she
was without the two smaller children, but then she caught
the sound of their whispering and giggling coming from
round the corner of the house.

Bernice looked up at Rachel with deliberate coyness,
while with the toe of her shoe she scraped an arc in the
gravel. She was holding a bunch of dahlias in her hand.

" Please, miss, would you like to buy some flowers? "
she asked with the ingratiating whine that she always
assumed for such occasions and that always gave Rachel
a peculiar feeling of distress. " Only two bob for the lot.
Look, miss, aren't they lovely? "

She held them out. There were seven or eight blooms,
of mixed sizes and colours.

" Where did you get them? " Rachel asked.

" From the garden," said Bernice.

" Whose garden? " Rachel asked brutally.

" My mum's garden," said Bernice quickly.

" What about the frost? " said Rachel. " It killed all
Miss Dalziel's dahlias. Didn't it kill your mother's? "

" Oh no, miss," said Bernice. " My mum's garden's
lovely."

Visualising the patch of neglected ground around the
Applins' shack, where nothing grew amongst the weeds
but a few discouraged potatoes that had probably sown

themselves from plants left by some earlier tenant, Rachel said, " Well, I'm afraid I don't want them."

She started to draw back.

" One and a tanner," the child offered swiftly.

" No thank you."

" Oh, please, miss! I got to sell 'em. My mum says so. I daren't go home till I sold 'em. I got to get the money. ' Don't you come back without the money,' she said, ' if you do I'll knock you into the middle of next week.' "

Bernice's face began to crumple, though her eyes were bright and watchful.

" No thank you," Rachel repeated.

But it was a sign of weakening that she did not immediately shut the door and the child saw it. Her voice developed a tremor.

" Mum needs the money ever so bad," she whimpered. " It's for the 'lectric. She hasn't got anything to put in the meter and it's terrible in this cold. And she can't cook dinner for the children. They're hungry and cold, miss."

The cold and hungry children, out of sight round the corner of the house, supported this statement with a burst of giggling.

" Now tell me," said Rachel, " does your mother even know what you're up to? "

A look of outrage appeared on Bernice's face.

" Oh, miss, she sent me out to get the money. She said to me, she said, ' Don't you come back without the money or I'll knock the living daylights out of you! '—and she will too, because of the poor little children." She thrust the flowers closer to Rachel. " A bob," she suggested.

Rachel sighed, fetched her handbag, found a shilling in it, gave it to Bernice and took the flowers.

She had known from the first that she was going to capitulate. She was never inclined to believe anything that Bernice told her, yet she could not keep out of her mind a picture of the Applin home, that decaying shack that ought to have been pulled down years ago. And since the father, as Rachel had been told by Mrs. Godfrey, who knew everything that went on in the village, squandered most of what he earned on the dogs, it was possible that there really was nothing to put in the electric meter in this horrible weather.

Besides, there was something about Bernice that touched Rachel. She took such good care of the two younger children. She trailed them around with her wherever she went. She was never harsh or shrill with them, giving them her love and protection in a world that had little use for them.

However, the gleam of satisfied cunning in Bernice's eyes as she clutched the shilling, gabbled some negligent thanks and shot off round the corner of the house, seemed to Rachel a complete betrayal of the fact that she had not been out on her mother's orders but engaged in private enterprise.

Putting the dahlias into a vase, Rachel carried them into the living-room. Jane had got up and was standing by the window, trying to see along the road to the cottage. But the garden wall cut off her view of all but a few yards of the road. She turned as Rachel came in again, murmured vaguely that the flowers were pretty and sat down again.

Rachel put the vase on the top of a bookcase.

" I've just weak-mindedly bought them from one of our local pests," she said and went on to tell Jane about the Applin family, who would be her very near neighbours if she and Roderick came to live in Miss Dalziel's barn.

It was easy to see that Jane was only half-listening. She was trying all the time to hear footsteps returning from the cottage.

It was about ten minutes later that they heard them, Roderick's and Paul's, coming rather slowly along the road, as if the two men had a good deal to talk over as they came. Even when they reached the house, they went on talking to each other in low voices in the hall. Then Paul came into the living-room by himself.

" I'm afraid we haven't found her or any clue to what's happened to her," he said. " We've searched the garden and the sheds and we've been down to the barn and asked Brian if he's seen or heard from her. No results. Roderick's going to do some telephoning now, to see if she's gone back to the London flat, or if one or two friends have heard anything from her. And if they haven't—if Roderick can't find out anything—then we're going to call the police."

He went to the fire and held out his hands to the warmth.

In the hall the telephone tinkled as Roderick picked it up. Jane started towards the door, then changed her mind and came back.

" You're being very good to us," she said to Paul. " I'm sorry we're being such a terrible bother."

" My dear child, I'm so sorry we can't help more," said Paul. " I won't deceive you—it looks to me as if that poor woman was attacked by someone and either—either was badly hurt and taken away, or at the best managed to get away herself and then probably collapsed somewhere. Because, if she wasn't seriously hurt, why hasn't anyone heard from her? Surely she'd have come here to us, or to Brian, or to someone in the village."

" Perhaps she's suffering from loss of memory," Jane suggested. With her eyes on the door, she was plainly listening more to the murmur of Roderick's voice on the telephone than to Paul.

" That charming woman," Paul muttered, staring into the fire. " So talented, so successful and at the same time so natural and friendly and unspoilt. She was kindness itself to us when we moved in here. And ever since, so hospitable, so delightful to meet. We live in a terrible world, a world that seems to be getting worse and worse. Or has it always been as terrible? Are things really worse, or is it only something to do with the way we look at them? "

Outside there was another tinkle on the telephone. Roderick was trying another number.

He tried several before he came into the room. His face had the expressionless look of someone in a state of shock. As Jane sprang out of her chair and went to him he put an arm round her and held her tight.

" I tried her flat first and didn't get any answer," he said. " Then I tried the Crosbys, the people who live in the basement flat. They haven't seen anything of her since Friday evening when they came up to have a drink with us. But they've got a key to Margot's flat, because they keep an eye on it for her when she's away, and they said they'd go up and see if there were any signs that she'd been back. While they were doing that I rang up my uncle. He doesn't know anything either. He told me about coming down yesterday and not getting any answer at the cottage and said that after a time he gave up and went home again. Then I rang up Tom Waterfield—he's the editor of *Worldwide*—just in case Margot had been in touch with him, but he said he hasn't heard anything from her since she got back from Geneva. Then I rang up the Crosbys again. . . ."

Roderick let go of Jane and started to come farther into the room, but suddenly gripped the back of a chair, sat down in it quickly and took his head in his hands.

After a moment he looked up at Jane.

" I'm sorry—this isn't what I thought we'd be doing to-day," he said.

She slid on to the arm of the chair beside him and drew his head against her.

" I suppose," said Paul, " the Crosbys didn't find anything in her flat."

" No," said Roderick. " Mrs. Crosby said the place had been left as tidy as Margot always leaves it—the bed made and so on. And they don't know anything about when she left, because they both go out to work on Saturday mornings and they're generally out of the place

39

before Margot's even got out of bed. But they think she must have left before lunch-time, because they can't remember hearing her walking about after they got back, and they do when she's there."

" So now we get in touch with the police, do we? " said Paul.

" I suppose we must. Jane——" Roderick took hold of one of her hands. " What do you think? If there's really nothing wrong, how furious will Margot be with us? "

She stirred uneasily. " I keep telling you, darling, she's never furious—I mean, never nastily."

" But if there's really some quite simple explanation of it all and she finds we've stirred up a lot of stupid publicity . . ." He paused. " No, I know there isn't any simple explanation. Yes, Mr. Hardwicke, let's get the police."

But he sounded so helpless about it that Paul said, " Would you like me to do it for you? I've had a certain amount of contact with our sergeant here."

" Oh—that's very good of you," said Roderick eagerly. " Are you sure you don't mind? I'm afraid we're putting you to an awful lot of trouble, but if you really wouldn't mind . . ."

" Gower's a very good chap," said Paul reassuringly. " I'll get him to come along first, then we'll talk over with him what we ought to do next."

He went out to the telephone.

When he came back he said that Sergeant Gower would meet them at the cottage as soon as he could get there.

Roderick and Jane stood up together. Again it struck Rachel that they were like two scared children, very close to each other in their distrust of the adult world and their reluctant dependence upon it.

As they went out, Paul looked at Rachel. " Coming too? " he asked.

She shook her head. " I'll stay and get some lunch ready. You'll all be pretty hungry by the time you're through. I'll have something waiting."

" Yes, that's a sensible idea," he said and followed Jane and Roderick.

Until the sound of their footsteps had faded down the road Rachel stayed where she was, standing near the fire. Then she went out to the kitchen. On her way she picked up her coat, and instead of starting to prepare a meal, went straight out into the garden. She went to the bottom of it, where there was a gap in the stone wall, through which it was easy to climb into the ploughed field behind the house, scrambled through and skirting the field, walked on until she came to a gap in the hedge that surrounded Miss Dalziel's garden. She pushed her way through it into the orchard and started across it to the barn.

CHAPTER V

RACHEL COULD see the old red roof of the barn and the plume of smoke from its chimney above the frosted branches of the fruit trees, but it was so long since these had been properly pruned that they had grown into a dense thicket, concealing most of the rest of the building. Brian Burden had subjected some of the trees to some well-intentioned hacking and sawing, but the results were hardly noticeable. As Rachel stumbled over some brambles in the rough grass, then caught her hair on the matted twigs of a plum tree, she thought wryly that going to visit Brian felt a little like trying to get to the palace of a Sleeping Beauty.

When he opened his door to her, he looked almost sleepy enough for the part, but he was not up to the mark in beauty. He was wearing a thick grey pullover and flannel trousers with a good deal of earth caked on to the knees. His hair was uncombed and he was unshaven.

Seeing Rachel, he mumbled an apology for his appearance.

"When I heard someone coming through the orchard," he said, "I thought it was probably some of the Applin tribe, who've a way of bursting in on one from all directions. Come in—if you don't mind the mess. I'm just having breakfast." Will you have some coffee?"

"I'd love some."

She was looking round. There was coffee in an earthenware jug on the rough wooden table, and a brown loaf and a half pound of butter, which was still in its paper wrapping. That seemed to be the whole of Brian's breakfast. Also on the table, which had been pulled close to the rusty, old-fashioned stove, were a typewriter and a pile of manuscript.

"You'll never be corrupted by luxury, living here, will you?" she said. "In this weather the place is hardly fit for human habitation."

"Luckily I don't much mind the cold," said Brian. He fetched a mug from a shelf and filled it with coffee. "And until this frosty spell started, I felt I was extremely well off. I've got the place to myself and I can do just what I like—work all night, if I want to and then have breakfast instead of lunch." He smiled at her as he handed her the mug. "Think of all those Applins, seven or eight of them, crowded into that shack, just as uncomfortable as this and no privacy to make up for it. Not that privacy is a thing they miss." He sat down at the table and picked up his own mug. "Have you ever been into that shack of theirs, Rachel? Sometimes there's some furniture in it, when the old man's done all right on the dogs. When he hasn't, it gets flogged around the village. And the things the children come cadging, the old clothes and so on—they don't get the use of them, they all go straight to the pawn shop in Fallford."

"You haven't much furniture yourself," said Rachel.

In the big, bare room, with roughly hewn beams supporting the high roof and a floor of uneven boards a foot wide, there were only the table, the two wooden chairs, a battered basket chair, a trunk and an iron bedstead.

" That's a matter of choice," said Brian. " There's less to sweep round. Besides, I'm free to leave when I feel like it."

" Oh, if you're thinking of leaving. . . ."

" I'm not," he said. " But it makes a difference that I can when I want to."

" I suppose so. And that's actually why I came over. I thought you ought to know. . . ." She hesitated, mainly because her own motives for coming had been very mixed and her knowledge of this suddenly confused her. " Brian, did you see that man yesterday evening, the one I told you I sent down here? "

" Margot's brother? "

" Yes."

" No, if he came, he didn't stay," said Brian.

" Or leave any message? "

" No."

" Well, I know what he came for," she said, " and it affects you. It seems Margot's decided to give this place to Roderick and the girl he's just married. Her brother, who's an architect, as you thought, was asked down to meet them and see what they'd like done to the barn to make it habitable. And they all seem to have forgotten there's someone living here already."

Brian went on looking at her for a moment after she had stopped, as if he thought that there was more coming. Then he put his mug down on the table, stared down into it and began to frown, as if he had noticed an insect floating about in the coffee.

" Oh well," he said at last.

" I—I thought you ought to know, in case no one else thought of warning you," she said.

" Yes. Thanks."

" The whole thing's made me feel rather angry."

" It doesn't matter—don't worry," he said.

She waited again, then said tentatively, " If you were beginning to think of leaving anyway, perhaps you won't mind much."

" As a matter of fact, I mind like hell," he said. " But it can't be helped. I've no rights over the place—none whatever. Who told you all this, Rachel? Margot herself? "

" No—haven't you heard about her? " she asked in surprise. " I thought you knew."

He gave a slight shake of his head.

" But I thought you saw my father and Roderick this morning," she said.

" Oh, that. Yes. They were looking for her. I told them I hadn't seen her."

" Didn't they tell you she's vanished, that we're all very worried? "

He looked up at her at last, then he got up, opened the top of the stove and began to stoke it with some chopped wood that was stacked beside it. For once, his slowness of response began to irritate Rachel.

" They're calling in the police," she said.

Without looking round, he asked her, " What do you mean by vanished? "

" She seems to have come down some time yesterday," she said, " probably on that morning train she usually takes when she comes for the week-end. She seems to have had a wash, put some flowers in a vase and some sherry and glasses on a tray, all in a hurry, as if she were expecting someone—and then just vanished."

Brian put the lid back on the stove. " I don't understand why you say vanished. Why shouldn't she just have gone away somewhere, perhaps with this person she was expecting? "

Rachel described the scene in the sitting-room of the cottage. She told him about the broken decanter, the overturned table, the stain on the carpet. As she did so she grew more and more uneasy at the fact that Brian still stood over the stove and did not look round at her.

With a kind of nervousness growing in her, she spoke more rapidly. " It looks quite horribly, you see, as if she'd been attacked, as if she'd fought and then—then either rushed out and escaped or got taken away." She stood up. " Now I ought to be getting home. I said I'd have some lunch waiting when Sergeant Gower's through with them."

" Wait a minute," said Brian slowly, almost cautiously, giving her the feeling, as he often did, that he was trying to work his way carefully and little by little through a complexity of impressions to some simple but important conclusion. " Rachel, this person Margot was expecting— have you any idea who it was? "

" None at all," she said, " unless it was her brother."

" You haven't got some idea in your head that it was me? "

He looked round at her then and their eyes met.

Rachel drew an unsteady breath. " Of course not," she said.

" Are you sure? " he asked.

" I told you," she said, " I haven't the faintest idea who it was."

" Because I was just wondering if—well, if that was really why you came over."

" I only came for the reason I told you, Brian." She said it over-emphatically because she was starting to feel that she had really had no good reason for coming, but had only, as usual, been helplessly drawn to him. " I thought someone ought to let you know what was being planned about this place."

" That was good of you," he said.

" But I suppose what they do now depends on what's happened to Miss Dalziel." She turned to the door.

He reached out and caught her by the arm. " Wait a

minute. Sit down. Listen. . . ." He thrust her back on to the chair by the stove. "Tell me, have they some idea this disappearance of Margot's was somehow connected with Roderick's marriage?"

"How odd—that's just what Jane asked me," said Rachel. "How could it be?"

"I don't know," said Brian. "I was just wondering. If Margot was upset enough about Roderick's marrying . . ."

"But she wasn't," said Rachel. "She was delighted."

"How do you know?"

"Jane told me so."

"I wonder if Jane would really know."

The way in which he spoke Jane's name caught Rachel's attention. "Do you know Jane, then?"

"Oh yes, I know her quite well," he said.

"She never said anything about knowing you when we were talking about the barn."

"No? Well, she's a forgetful creature." He said it with sardonic gentleness. "It'll be a curious sort of marriage. I should think Roderick fell in love with her because she's about the only woman he's met who doesn't frighten him."

"I'd never have thought Roderick was frightened of women," said Rachel. "I've always thought of him as one of those quietly ruthless people who'd generally arrange to do just what he wanted with anyone else—man or woman."

"Oh yes, he's ruthless," said Brian, "but mainly because he's frightened. It's Margot's doing. You have to be very tough to cope with her."

"Is Jane very tough, then, because she seems to feel she can cope?"

He considered that. "Yes, in her own way she is tough, staggeringly tough—mainly because so little ever really touches her. And she has a completely imaginary picture of Margot in her mind, mainly because Margot's about as unlike Jane's parents as she could be. Her father's a Brigadier and her mother's a J.P., and when no one's around they drink too much gin and start throwing things and cursing at one another—or so Jane says. Her hatred of them is about her most stable emotion. It's almost a kind of loyalty."

"Then I can see Miss Dalziel would be a pleasant change. She's so calm and good tempered."

"But have you ever looked at her profile?" Brian asked. "People's profiles often give away all sorts of things about them they know how to hide when they're looking straight at you. Margot's profile is like a little Caesar's."

"You sound as if you don't much like her," said Rachel.

His gaze strayed absently from her face to the pile of manuscript on the table.

"Oh, I like her," he said. "She's been uncommonly good to me and I'm grateful—really far more grateful than I probably sound. If I'd gone on much longer in that insurance office I'd have taken to drink, but if I hadn't had this place as a bolt-hole, I don't suppose I'd really have had the courage to break away. All the same, I'd always be scared of any close relationship with Margot. I think Roderick gets his ruthlessness from her side of the family."

Rachel was still puzzling over what Brian had said earlier. "Brian, what did you really mean when you asked if Margot's disappearance could be connected with Roderick's marriage? Did you mean you were afraid it was Roderick who—who was there with her yesterday?"

"No!" Brian said, sharply, then looked disconcerted at his own vehemence. "I was just fumbling around, Rachel. And I shouldn't have been, because it's a wonderful way of starting up suspicions, which is unforgivable at a time like this. And actually I wasn't thinking of Roderick at all. I was just wondering if Margot herself . . ."

He stopped as someone knocked at the door.

As Brian went towards it, Rachel stood up and moved nearer to the stove. She thought that this was very likely her father, who had returned home with Roderick and Jane, found neither Rachel nor any lunch waiting and come impatiently to look for her. And he would not be at all pleased at finding her here and on the way home with her he would make some edged remarks about the way that Brian had stayed talking to her, instead of showing some concern for Miss Dalziel by going to the cottage to see if he could help.

And Rachel would say nothing. She would find her thoughts locked up in a helpless, angry silence, while she longed somehow to get away from the person she had loved most all her life.

Brian opened the door.

An adenoidal voice, not in the least like Paul Hardwicke's, said, " Morning, Mr. Burden."

Brian did not answer at once. Then, as if reluctantly, he said, " Hallo, Kevin."

" Cold morning."

" Pretty cold," said Brian.

" No sign of a thaw to-day."

" No."

Brian added nothing to that and there was a silence, during which Kevin shuffled his feet on the path and Brian remained squarely in the doorway, obviously waiting for him to go. There had been nothing in Brian's voice that invited Kevin to explain himself.

With a rush of words, Kevin suddenly went on, " Listen, Mr. Burden, I got to talk to you. I got to explain about last night. There's going to be trouble now and unless you stand by me and keep what I told you to yourself I'm going to be in it. And I don't want any part of it. I was nowhere near the place. I was with my friends. They can prove it. Only who's going to believe them if you speak up against me. . . ? "

He stopped abruptly as Rachel came forward towards the door.

For an instant Kevin's face blazed with anger, then he managed the ingratiating Applin smile. " Sorry," he said. " Didn't know you had company, Mr. Burden."

" Don't worry," said Rachel. " I'm just leaving."

Kevin was already half-way along the path, but as she passed Brian and came out of the door he paused and looked back at her. He was a sturdily built youth with his family's thick black hair, black eyes and healthy ruddy cheeks, and the heavy grace of a young cart-horse. In spite of his tapered trousers, pointed shoes and short overcoat of shiny, imitation black leather, he had a look of wholesomeness and strength.

" Didn't mean to butt in, I can come back later," he mumbled. But he did not go on to the gate. Looking at Brian, he went on. " Didn't see a car, so I thought you was alone."

There was a flat deliberateness in his voice as he said it. He smiled again and a sly look of challenge came into his bright eyes.

Brian frowned and his slow voice sounded unusually sullen. " All right, come in if you want to, Kevin. But, Rachel, there's no need for you to go."

" Well," said Kevin, walking slowly back until he was once more facing Brian in the doorway, " what I was wanting was a private talk like. But if it's inconvenient, like I said, I can come another time."

" I ought to go home," said Rachel. " They may all be back there, waiting for something to eat."

" I suppose so," said Brian. " All right. But I'll come round presently. Or I'll go up to the cottage, to see if there's anything I can do. Or—or something."

" Yes, do," said Rachel, puzzled by what had happened, disturbed by it and now wanting to get away, for Kevin's healthy look, his bright, friendly black eyes and his ugly history of violence, gave her a sick feeling of revulsion.

As she pushed her way in among the brambles and fruit trees again, she wondered unhappily what there was between him and Brian and why, when Kevin had said that he thought Brian must be alone because there had been no car outside, had Brian at once given in to him and told him to stay.

CHAPTER VI

IT WAS about three o'clock that afternoon when Detective-Inspector Walter Creed, sent from Fallford to look into the disappearance of Margot Dalziel, got out of his car at the new red brick house of Sergeant Gower and walked slowly up the path to the door with the police sign above it. Looking at the damage done to the Gowers' chrysanthemums by the frost, he wondered why it should have been so bad here when his own garden in Fallford had hardly suffered. But that was the way of things. One was spared and another taken. It happened all the time, like with those two boys who had been up in court last week for stealing a car, after knocking out the driver and leaving him, for all they knew, to die by the roadside. One of them had gone to gaol, while the other had got off with a relatively light fine and a month to pay it in. It was all highly mysterious. There was no telling nowadays where mercy would strike, any more than the frost.

Creed was a tall man, wiry and lean. His close-clipped hair was mottled grey and brown. His bony face, on which the skin looked as if it were slightly too small a fit, so that it was always drawn into a number of tight wrinkles, was covered with large freckles. His eyes were grey-green, flecked with brown. They were the shrewd but rather evasive eyes of a man who was determined that nothing should matter to him too much. Creed had once been a very ambitious police officer, but years ago had realised that he had gone as far as he was ever going. The effort to accept that knowledge about himself had not been small. Forcing himself to go on doing his work conscientiously, he had tried to keep some hopefulness for retirement, which might in some ways be a rather frightening thought, but at least made most men equal, or nearly.

He was whistling softly when Gower opened the door. Gower was a quiet, brisk man who also had no hope of further promotion, but whose work contentedly filled his life. He seldom wasted time. He had already made certain inquiries in the village and as the two men started out for Miss Dalziel's cottage, he began to tell Creed what he had done since telephoning his report to Fallford. He had questioned the station-master and the one porter at the station to ask if they had seen Miss Dalziel get off any train the day before. Neither of them, he said, remembered having seen her. He had spoken to the owner of the one taxi in the village, to ask if he had driven Miss Dalziel home from the station. The taxi-driver had said that he had not. Gower had also put a call through to the bus-depot, although Miss Dalziel's nephew had told him that she never came down by bus, and the bus people were looking into the matter.

" But it's certain she did come down sometime yesterday, is it? " said Creed.

" They all think she did," said Gower. " Her nephew and her neighbours. They think she got in about mid-day."

" Then the chances are she came by car," said Creed.

" She could have, only no one saw it—not in the day-time. They saw her brother's later, like I told you on the phone, but no one remembers seeing a car stop at her house before that."

" I see." Creed had just stopped his car at the gate of Margot Dalziel's cottage and was looking at its trim thatch, its white walls with its pattern of dark timber, its rose-grown porch. " Pretty place," he said. " The day-dream home of an awful lot of people, Jim."

" Not mine," said Gower. " Bump your head wherever you go."

" Still, these old places have got something. When I retire . . ."

Creed stopped himself. He never intended to let the subject of retirement slip into his conversation nearly as often as it did. He knew that it didn't sound too good. Pushing open the gate, he walked up the path to the door of the cottage.

Before he reached it, it was opened by Paul Hardwicke.

" I've left the young people next door," said Paul. " They're very upset and I didn't think sitting about here, waiting for you, was going to do them any good. They're with my daughter, who's very capable. I thought probably you could talk to them over there, but if you'd like to see them here, I'll fetch them."

" Thanks," said Creed. " We'll think about that presently. I think I'll start by looking round and seeing what's led you to think there's something wrong about this absence of Miss Dalziel's."

" Come in here then," said Paul, " and mind your head." He ducked to go through the low doorway into the stitting-room.

Creed followed him and stood in the middle of the room, unconsciously keeping his head slightly bent. It would not really have reached the ceiling if he had stood upright, yet the dark beams felt uncomfortably close. He looked round slowly, observing, memorising.

She had some nice things, he thought. All those books in that bookcase, with their old leather bindings and the dim gilt of their titles. They were something that he would have liked to own himself. He had always had a fancy for well-bound books and had tried, for a short time, to collect a few. But he had given it up pretty quickly on finding out how expensive it came. Now he stuck to paperbacks.

Miss Dalziel must be a fairly wealthy woman, he

decided, or else one of the lucky ones who had inherited their treasures. That rug, all crumpled up and stained with the spilled sherry, looked a good one. And those long-stemmed roses were not what he would ever have thought of taking home except for a very special occasion. But perhaps there had been a very special occasion. . . .

He went on looking thoughtfully at the roses, then picked up and looked through the contents of the hand-bag that had fallen on the floor. There were all the usual things that women carry, and about forty pounds in a note-case.

" Her money's still here," he said.

" So her nephew told me," said Paul.

" Well, let me see the rest of it."

Paul took him round the cottage, upstairs and down-stairs and then out into the garden.

" Yes, I see," Creed said from time to time, as if he were agreeing that there was cause here for worry about the disappearance of Margot Dalziel.

Back in the cottage after looking in the toolshed and the garage, he returned to the small, modernised kitchen and while Paul and Gower watched from the doorway, he prowled around, looking into the cupboards, the refriger-ator, the bread-bin, the plastic refuse-bucket under the sink.

" Empty," he said. " Everything practically empty. It looks as if all she had time to do when she got in was put her roses in water and get out the drinks."

" She lit the fire too," said Gower.

" That's right," said Creed. " Would you say that was normal, Mr. Hardwicke? "

Paul raised one eyebrow to show that he had not understood the question.

" I was thinking," said Creed, " that when my wife and I go home after we've been away somewhere, we generally stop on the way and buy a few supplies—bread, some chops, some tomatoes—you know what I mean.

But there's no bread in that bin there, and there's only butter and eggs and a few odds and ends in the fridge, the sort of things that might have been there for weeks. So I was wondering what Miss Dalziel meant to do about getting in food for her week-end."

" I don't know," said Paul. " I've no idea what she usually did. It's the sort of thing my daughter might be able to tell you. Or perhaps young Dalziel would know."

" Didn't she have any domestic help here? " Creed asked. " Didn't anyone clean the place and keep an eye on it for her? "

" Well, I suppose you could say Mr. Burden keeps an eye on it. He lives in the old barn at the bottom of the orchard. But domestic help . . ." Paul tried hard to remember what he had been told on this matter, feeling that he had probably been told a great deal. All women talked about their domestic help. But the subject had never seemed to him sufficiently interesting for him to listen carefully when it came up. " I think a woman from the village comes in sometime during the week and cleans up. Again, my daughter . . ."

" Mrs. Brooke," said Gower. " Comes in Mondays and Fridays, two-thirty to five."

" Thanks, Jim," said Creed. " Fridays. So the place would have been swept and dusted and the fire laid and so on, the day before Miss Dalziel got home."

" Yes," said Paul.

" But no supplies bought."

" So it seems."

" So Miss Dalziel must have thought she'd have time, after getting here, to go to the shops and buy some food for the week-end."

" Ah, I see what you mean," said Paul. " You're trying to fix the time she got here. My daughter can tell you about that too. We've worked it out that Miss Dalziel probably arrived on the eleven-forty-five and got to the cottage about twelve o'clock. You see, I was round here a bit earlier in the morning and saw a milk-bottle on the doorstep. The birds had pecked a hole through the top, so when I told my daughter about it, she said she'd bring round a fresh bottle for Miss Dalziel. But when she got here with it, a little after twelve o'clock, the bottle had been taken in. I think that fixes the time fairly certainly, doesn't it? "

" But your daughter didn't actually see Miss Dalziel, did she? " said Creed.

" She didn't try to," said Paul. " She was in rather a hurry and she didn't stay. But you'd better ask her about that yourself."

The tight wrinkles on Creed's thin face seemed to deepen. " The unsatisfactory part in your calculations, you see, Mr. Hardwicke, is that there's no bottle of milk in that fridge."

Paul stared at him blankly for a moment. Then he went to the refrigerator and looked inside it.

" No," he said. " You're quite right, Inspector. What does that mean? "

Creed did not answer.

" Perhaps she simply drank the milk," said Paul, " though I don't know, of course, if she's one of the people who toss off milk by the pint."

" Still, wouldn't she have kept a little for tea or coffee later?" said Creed.

" I suppose so," said Paul.

" And what did she do with the empty bottle? "

" She might have put it back on the doorstep."

Creed sat down on one of the plastic-seated kitchen chairs.

" Wouldn't it have been very curious behaviour," he said, " when she's in such a hurry to get ready for her visitor that she doesn't unpack, doesn't hang up her coat, or anything of that kind, to drink off a whole pint of milk and put the bottle back on the doorstep? "

The sergeant cleared his throat and made a suggestion. " Perhaps it was her assailant done it," he said.

" Wouldn't that be odder still? " said Paul.

" Well, I don't know," said Gower. " People do queer things. Take that chap who shot several people in a bungalow, then opened a can of soup and sat down and drank it off on the spot."

" True," said Creed. " Criminals have to keep up their strength, the same as other people. Violence takes it out of you. It's an idea, Jim."

Paul gave him a worried glance, trying to make out how seriously he had spoken. The speckled, grey-green eyes did not tell him much.

Creed went on, " When was the last time you saw Miss Dalziel, Mr. Hardwicke? "

" Just a fortnight ago," said Paul. " She was down here for the week-end, and my daughter and I came over for a drink with her about six o'clock. She was returning to London next day, she told us, and later in the week she was going to Geneva for a conference of some sort. She travelled a great deal in connection with her work, you know. She was——" He was horrified at the lapse. " She *is* a very remarkable and brilliant woman."

" With a good many friends, I suppose," said Creed.

" Oh yes, certainly."

" And some enemies? "

" I'm afraid I don't know about that. But I imagine . . ." Paul hesitated and Creed thought suddenly that if the man said again that his daughter would know, it would be time to pick up that handsome stainless steel frying-pan over there and bring it smartly down on the fine, stupid, white head.

Only a momentary gleam in Creed's eyes betrayed this impulse, and Paul did not notice it. He said reflectively, " I imagine she must have had enemies. A woman of that sort, who's fought her way up to a very high position in the journalistic world, can't have done it without—well, treading on a few corns on the way."

" Or even cutting a few throats, perhaps? "

Paul smiled uneasily. " I suppose so. Yet she's a charming woman. Small, rather fragile in appearance—very feminine, if you know what I mean. Not at all aggressive or domineering—anyway, in her private life. But extremely vital, of course. And capable. One always felt that."

" Is there a picture of her anywhere? " asked Creed.

" I believe her nephew has one."

" Then perhaps I'd better get on and talk to him now."

Creed stood up. He put his hands in his pockets, bent his head to dodge the lintel, and went out by the back door into the garden. The two other men followed him.

As they walked round the cottage to the car, Creed started to think about the other time that he had come here, when he had had to question the family of the boy who had been arrested for beating up the old woman in the cigarette shop in Fallford. The parents had been prepared to lie themselves blue in the face to give the boy an alibi and had been too slow-witted to realise that since the woman's screams had been heard by the man on the beat and the boy had walked out of the shop with the money from the till in his pockets, straight into the arms of Constable Dicker, a perjured alibi was not going to help him much.

" That Applin boy," Creed said to Gower, " he's home again, isn't he? "

" That's right," said Gower. " Came home this week."

" Better look into what he was doing yesterday, then."

And very likely, thought Creed, as they got into the car and drove the thirty yards or so to the Hardwickes' gate, that was as far as they would have to look, even if there was something queer about the money left in the handbag. That didn't really sound like Kevin Applin.

At the Hardwickes' house, Creed saw Roderick first, upstairs in Mr. Hardwicke's study. Roderick was white-faced, tense and restless. He smoked all the time and although his answers to Creed's questions were clear and direct, his eyes looked dazed and when they met Creed's, were filled with blank confusion.

Creed thought that here was someone who had already made up his mind that the worst had happened.

" When did you last see your aunt, Mr. Dalziel? " Creed asked him.

The photograph of her that Roderick had given him lay on the table between them. It was a colour-print of a small, smiling woman in a full-skirted summer dress, with a flock of pigeons at her feet. Roderick had said that it had been taken the summer before in Regent's Park. She looked a good deal younger than Creed had expected, although her short, curly hair was grey. What struck him most about her was her air of gay vitality and the obvious fact that she knew how to pose for the camera.

In the soft, level voice that he used throughout the interview, Roderick answered, " On Friday evening, Inspector."

" Where was that? "

" In her flat in London. It's near Parliament Hill Fields." Roderick gave the address and Gower made a note of it. " She'd been to Geneva to a conference and I went to London Airport to meet her and drive her home. We had a drink in her flat—the people from the flat below came up and joined us—then she and I went out for dinner together. Then I drove her home again and stayed till—oh, about half past ten, I think. That's the last time . . ." The sentence faded.

" Was your wife with you? " Creed asked.

" No, she'd gone down to stay with her parents," said Roderick. " Perhaps I ought to explain all that. Perhaps it'll be best if I tell you what the situation was. We got married secretly last Tuesday, while my aunt was away. It's difficult now to say just why we did, except that we both wanted to avoid fuss. My wife's parents would probably have wanted a village wedding with all the trimmings. Margot wouldn't have bothered about that— she was always far too busy—all the same, I'd got an idea she'd be against the marriage, might try to make us put it off, or something."

Roderick lit a fresh cigarette from the stub of the last and inhaled deeply while Creed and Gower waited.

" As I said, it's fearfully difficult now to remember why I was so sure of it," Roderick went on," except that over the years she's had a way of arranging my life for me. Very benevolently, of course, and generally wisely. But here was something I simply didn't want to have to discuss with her. I'm out of a job, for one thing, and I could imagine her telling me we ought to wait at least until I'd got something definite fixed up. But I'd saved some money—I worked as a courier for a travel agency all the summer and lived on expenses and didn't spend my salary—so that was all right, I thought, and I didn't want to have to listen to a lot of common sense. I've always given in when I've done that."

Roderick's mouth twitched in a little nervous smile.

" And what was Miss Dalziel's reaction? " Creed asked.

" Oh, Jane was right, she was delighted," said Roderick.

" When did you tell her? "

" On the drive back from the airport. I hadn't meant to meet her, but Jane insisted I should. She was going down to see her parents on Friday and break the news to them and then I was to follow on Saturday and be introduced to them. And before she went off she somehow persuaded me to go and meet Margot. . . ." The calm voice shook slightly.

" Did she tell you anything about her plans for the week-end? " Creed asked.

" Yes, she told me she was coming down here next day."

" Did she mention how—by train, car, bus? "

" I don't think so, but she generally came by train. She hadn't a car herself. She always said you could take all the taxis you could ever want for half the cost of running a car."

" And she was expecting you and your wife to-day, was she? "

" Yes. Jane's parents live the other side of Fallford, you see, only about twenty-five miles away."

Creed nodded, fiddling with a pencil on the table before him.

" You come here fairly often, I believe," he said.

" Oh yes."

" Have you a key to the cottage? "

" Yes."

" So you let yourself in this morning? "

" Yes."

" And found everything just as it is now? "

" Yes."

" You don't know if anything in the cottage is missing?"

Roderick shook his head. " I haven't noticed anything."

" Now, there's something else I'd like you to tell me about," said Creed. " Those roses. It's obvious they came from a florist, not out of somebody's garden. So what do you think happened—did she buy them herself on the way here, because this visitor she was expecting was someone a bit special, or was it the visitor who brought them for her? "

" I think she probably bought them for herself," said Roderick. " She often did that. She was mad about flowers. She made me stop and buy some chrysanthemums from a shop on the way back to her flat from the airport."

" I see," said Creed. " Now can you tell me something about your own movements between the time you left Miss Dalziel on Friday evening and your arrival here? "

Roderick gave a resigned sort of nod. The question, Creed saw, had caused neither surprise nor resentment. It had been expected. Yet as soon as Roderick tried to answer it, he seemed to lose his way and to need a moment of fierce puffing at his cigarette before he could go on.

" I told you, didn't I, I left her about half past ten? " he said. " I went home to the room I live in—22 Worsley

Gardens, off Judd Street, and I was there till about half past twelve next day—or perhaps a quarter to one—when I went to have lunch at Cirio's place in the Euston Road. Then I went back, got my bag and the car and drove down to my wife's home. I think it was about half past four when I got there. And I was there until we left this morning—about eleven o'clock. And then we drove straight here."

"Thank you," said Creed. "That's very clear and helpful. Now I'd be grateful if you'd ask Mrs. Dalziel to come in."

Roderick stiffened in his chair and his air of helplessness vanished. "Is that necessary, Inspector? She's very upset."

"You can be present, if you wish," said Creed. "I don't expect I'll have to keep her long."

"I see. Well, I'll see how she feels about it." Roderick stood up and went out.

Waiting for Jane, Creed picked up the photograph and looked at it carefully, studying the laughing face of Margot Dalziel. An attractive woman, he thought, and wondered why she had never married. It could hardly have been for lack of chances. She was by no means only an intellectual type, nor a mere fashion-plate either. He supposed that he ought to buy a copy of that magazine she worked for and see if he could pick up any clues about her from the sort of stuff she wrote. But it would probably be a bit over his head, sociology and so forth. It might only confuse him. He laid the photograph down again as Jane came in.

She went quickly to the chair that Roderick had left a few minutes before, sat down on the edge of it, folded her arms on the table, gave Creed a smile that struck him as, in the circumstances, amazingly cheerful, and said, brightly, "Well, here I am, Inspector. Incidentally, I expect you know my mother. She's Mrs. Meredith."

That jolted Creed. Certainly he knew Mrs. Meredith,

who was just about the most formidably capricious J.P. he had ever had to deal with. A grenadier of a woman, who always looked, on the bench, as if she were longing to send off to hard labour even the forgetful motorist who had parked without lights, she was in fact subject to attacks of what to Creed was an absolutely incomprehensible tolerance. The case of the incorrigible drunk, of the prostitute picked up for soliciting, of the man who was trying to dodge the payments that he had been ordered to make to the wife he had abandoned, would seem all of a sudden to fill Mrs. Meredith with a desperate conviction that there, but for the grace of God, went she. But only on certain days. On other days she could be as hard as the worst of them. There was no principle in it, that Creed had ever been able to observe.

"Yes, I know Mrs. Meredith," he said sombrely. "Now would you mind telling me when you last saw Miss Dalziel?"

"Oh, it was ages ago," said Jane. "About three weeks. She took Roderick and me to the theatre. She thought, you see, that she was throwing us together. She kept doing it and he let her go on thinking that he was simply not aware of my existence. And all the time we were practically engaged—only that doesn't exactly describe it, of course. We never were *engaged*. We just went and got married." Her smile disappeared. "It seems rather mean now."

"You didn't see Miss Dalziel, or even talk with her on the telephone after she got back from Geneva on Friday?" Creed asked.

"No," said Jane.

"How was that?"

"Well, I'd gone home," she said. "I had to break the news of my marriage to my parents."

"I see. And were you at home the whole week-end?"

"More or less."

"And that means?"

" Oh, that I—I didn't get down there until about seven on Friday evening. I didn't get away from my job till five, then I went to Waterloo and caught the five-forty to Fallford and Daddy met me there with the car and so I got home about seven. And we had drinks straight away and dinner, and I told Mummy and Daddy about marrying Roderick and that I'd asked him down next day, and mercifully they didn't take it too badly. Then I had a bath and believe it or not, the water was practically ice-cold, as it nearly always is, because if you stoke the fire too much, it boils. You'd think that nowadays people would have the sense to do something about a thing like that, wouldn't you? There isn't any actual virtue in being uncomfortable, though Mummy sometimes seems to think——"

Creed interrupted, " And next day? "

" Next day Roderick came down," she said.

" But before he came," said Creed. " He didn't arrive till the afternoon, did he? "

She put a hand quickly to her mouth.

" No," she said, letting her hand drop again. " He got there for tea. It was about half past four, I think. And we spent all the rest of the day with my parents. Roderick did a lot of odd jobs for Mummy and had a long talk about finance with Daddy and it all went off simply wonderfully. I never felt so happy in my life. But now . . . now . . ."

" Before your husband arrived," said Creed, " did you spend the whole day at home? "

" Oh yes—except that I took the car and went for a short drive in the morning. I did a little shopping for Mummy in Fallford."

" I see. Thank you."

" Is that all? " she asked and got to her feet so quickly and went out so promptly that Creed barely had time to ask her if she would mind sending Miss Hardwicke to see him.

Turning to Gower when she had gone, he said, " Odd, that, wasn't it, Jim? She didn't like those last questions. What do you make of that? "

" Maybe her mother didn't know about her taking the car out and she's afraid we'll let on," said Gower.

" Or was it that she didn't really know how Dalziel spent the day before he turned up there for tea? "

" Ah, maybe," said Gower, nodding.

" What d'you think—could he have had lunch when he said he did in the Euston Road, then come all the way here—it's about ninety miles, isn't it?—gone back on his tracks through Fallford to the Merediths' house, and still got there at half past four? "

" No," said Gower, " specially if he brought Miss Dalziel here with him, did her in and got rid of the body."

" Well, she got here somehow and we still don't know how," said Creed.

" Only, if that's how it was," said Gower, " it couldn't have been her who took the bottle of milk in in the morning."

" No," said Creed.

Frowning, Gower reached for the photograph and drew it towards him.

" Made up your mind she's dead, haven't you? " he said as he stared at the woman's bright, smiling face.

" Don't you think so yourself? " said Creed.

" Yes," said Gower flatly.

The starkness of the answer bothered Creed and immediately made him want to find reasons for doubting his own conclusions. Only for the moment he could not think of anything much in the way of a reason. He believed that Margot Dalziel was dead and thought that in spite of some odd things that hadn't been explained yet, such as how she had got to the cottage, and for whom she had so hurriedly brought out the sherry, and who had bought the yellow roses, Kevin Applin was almost certainly the murderer. He had probably left the money in the handbag through sheer muddle and panic.

" Well, you never know," he said. " She may walk in alive and kicking any moment now."

The door opened. A woman walked in. But it was not the woman of the photograph. It was only Rachel Hardwicke, who said, as she went to the chair where Roderick and Jane had sat, " I'm sorry to have been so long, but my father and I decided Mr. and Mrs. Dalziel had better not spend the night at the cottage, as things are, and that they'd better stay here. So while you were talking to Mr. Dalziel, we went along to fetch their luggage, and I've only just got back."

" They seem to be remarkably lucky in their neighbours," said Creed. " Now, Miss Hardwicke, will you tell me about that business of the milk-bottle. I've been hearing about it from other people, but I'd like to hear it from you. I'd like to know just what time you went round to the cottage and saw it was gone. And I'd like to know if there wasn't anything else—anything at all—some sound inside the house perhaps, or a shadow across a window, that would help us to decide whether or not Miss Dalziel had arrived and was the person who took in that bottle of milk."

Rachel had sat down in the chair facing him.

" I'm sorry," she said. " I didn't notice anything. It was a bit after twelve o'clock when I got there and when I saw the bottle had been taken in, I just went straight on to the village."

" You didn't ring or knock? "

He saw a look of distress on her face. " No, I didn't. Miss Dalziel was an awfully hospitable person and she'd almost certainly have asked me in for some sherry, and I was never very good at saying no to her about anything, and I happened to be in a hurry, so—so I just went on."

" And you can't remember hearing anything inside? "

" No," she said.

" Or seeing anything? You must have passed fairly close to the sitting-room window. You didn't notice anything unusual? "

" No, I don't think I even looked at the windows," she said. " They're fairly small, you know, and the walls are very thick and the room's rather dark. So I don't suppose I'd have seen anything inside, even if I'd looked."

" But you're sure about the milk-bottle? It was on the doorstep when your father went there at about eleven-fifteen, and it was gone by the time you arrived about an hour later."

" Yes," she said.

Creed thanked her and said that was all for the present. That milk bottle, he thought, looked like being the most important thing in the case.

All of a sudden he felt sure that he knew where it was. It was somewhere in the rough grass of Margot Dalziel's orchard. He saw clearly what must have happened. He saw Kevin Applin prowling around the cottage, looking for what he could pick up, then being surprised by Margot Dalziel and lashing out murderously in rage and fear, and then sitting down and drinking the pint of milk and hurling the empty bottle away into the long grass behind the cottage, while he made up his slow mind what to do with the body. So the thing to do now, even before the orders for a general search went out, was to take a quick look in the orchard. . . .

Creed became aware of a mounting excitement. But as soon as he became aware of it, it died. This had happened too late. Too late for even an outstanding success to make any difference to him. You couldn't expect promotion when you had only two more years to go and mere commendation had a way of leaving a surprisingly bitter taste behind it.

Standing up and pocketing the photograph of Margot Dalziel, he said tersely, " Come on, Jim, I think we've finished here for the moment and I want to go back again next door."

But as it turned out, there was no empty milk-bottle in the orchard.

For a little while Creed clung stubbornly to the idea that he would find it in another moment, then suddenly found himself wondering why in the world he had thought his idea so damned brilliant.

This was just the sort of way he had gone wrong over and over again in the past. He had always fallen for his own bright ideas and believed in them blindly until the total lack of foundation for them jolted him back to reason. Then he had always had a humiliated feeling of resentment at having to get back on to the well-trodden path of routine. From that point on in a case he had always felt more or less a failure, a plodding, unimaginative policeman who was scared to look beyond the end of his nose.

Routine now meant a report back to Fallford, the spreading of the news of the woman's disappearance through the usual channels, the sending out of search parties. A dreary business. A chore that had been done so many times before and would no doubt be done a good many times more in the remaining two years.

With a look of remarkable detachment on his face, Creed got into his car and drove away.

CHAPTER VII

THAT EVENING a police notice on television spread the news of Margot Dalziel's disappearance and was heard by Paul and Rachel in the living-room. But Roderick and Jane had already gone up to bed in the Hardwickes' spare bedroom, sent up at an unusually early hour by Paul, who had taken a very strong line on their need of rest after their day of anxiety.

When he had got rid of them, he said to Rachel, " They wouldn't have wanted to sit on here with us, hashing things over and over, or else trying to talk as if there were nothing wrong. I'm not sure which they'd have thought the more proper thing to do, but either would have been a strain—for me too, I admit. I'm very sorry about it, but I find sympathy a very wearing emotion."

" So are some others," said Rachel absently.

The emotion that had worn at her nerves all the afternoon and evening was worry because Brian had not come over, as she thought that he had promised just before she left the barn. There was something uncomfortably chilling about such indifference to the fate of Miss Dalziel, even if it was the truth that he had no great regard for her. Also Rachel had not been able to stop thinking about the strange little scene between Brian and Kevin. She felt sure that whatever Kevin had wanted to tell Brian in private had been somehow connected with what had happened in the cottage. But had Brian said anything about it to the police?

Seeing her father looking at her curiously, she reached out and turned a knob on the television. Music filled the room for a little while, then came the news and the police message.

As the announcer concluded " . . . and it is feared that she may be wandering, suffering from loss of memory," Rachel turned the switch off and stood up.

" Only they don't really fear that, do they? " she said, yawning as she went to the door. " They seemed to me to be very sure she's dead."

" If she isn't," said Paul, " a loss of memory is almost the only other possibility. Where are you going? Not to bed already, are you? Stay and let's talk quietly for a little while. Please do, my dear, I need it. I'm terribly on edge."

" I was going to wash up," said Rachel. " I've been letting it accumulate all day and there's an awful lot of it."

" All right, let's do it together, then," said Paul.

" It's a soothing occupation if you take it slowly. Then I'll make us a nightcap."

He followed her out to the kitchen.

Only realising how tired she was as she started to tidy it, stacking the dishes from the day's meals in the sink, Rachel said wearily, " It's a queer thing—there's something that detective asked me that I can't get out of my mind and yet thinking about it isn't the least use, because I really don't remember anything odd. . . ."

But Paul, standing waiting with dishcloth in hand, was pursuing a line of thought of his own.

" Suppose she was attacked—not killed—and left unconscious there in that room," he said, " and then came to and couldn't remember anything and went wandering off. That is a possibility, you know. It could have happened."

Rachel turned on the hot tap and poured detergent into the water.

" I wonder what sort of person Miss Dalziel really was—is—was," she said. " I wonder, I mean, if Roderick wasn't right about her."

Paul picked up the glass that she put down on the draining board.

" Right in what way about her? " he asked.

" He probably knew her better than anyone," said Rachel. " Don't you think so? "

" I expect so."

" And he was terrified of her stopping his marriage."

" Only he seems to have been quite mistaken there."

" Yes." Rachel frowned into the steaming foam. " But was he really? "

Paul held the glass up to the light, detected a smear and resumed polishing.

" It's true we've only his word for it," he said. " You know, Rachel, that hadn't occurred to me. It's an interesting thought."

" That isn't what I meant," she said. " I was thinking

that if Roderick was right that Miss Dalziel would have hated the idea of his getting married and might actually have tried to stop it if she'd had a chance, and then—then if she'd found she was too late to stop it, she might—well, mightn't she?—have decided to have a sort of revenge. You see, the more I think about it, the more I feel there's something wrong about that scene in the cottage."

It took Paul a moment to take in what Rachel was suggesting. Then he exclaimed, " Good God, what an atrocious thought! You aren't serious, are you? "

Rachel did not know quite how serious she was.

" It isn't any more atrocious than the thought of murder," she said.

" Except you're making out it's Miss Dalziel who's the criminal," said Paul. " You're making out that a woman like that—my God, just think of it!—a gifted, charming, generous-minded woman, could—could fake a horrible scene like that and disappear, just to cause as much unhappiness as possible to those two young people."

" But is she really charming and generous-minded? " said Rachel. " That's what I'm wondering."

Paul put the glass down carefully, so carefully that it looked as if he had suddenly become afraid of what he might do with it if it remained in his hands.

" Has she ever given you the slightest cause to think otherwise? " he asked.

" I don't think so," said Rachel. " But even if she hasn't, that doesn't mean she mightn't, sooner or later. It would take one ages to get to know everything about a woman like that. She isn't exactly simple and obvious and I should think she'd be pretty good at making one think whatever she wanted one to think about her."

Paul gave his head a fierce shake. " A woman like that! " he echoed, as if the phrase particularly riled him.

" Well, Roderick probably really knows a lot about her," said Rachel, " and he was afraid of her."

" But what you're suggesting would mean she was a lunatic."

" A sort of one, I suppose. At least that she'd had a breakdown, perhaps because the news of Roderick's marriage upset her so badly, when she was already tired out after that conference in Geneva. She always lived at terrifically high speed, didn't she? "

" But you've no evidence at all that the news did upset her," said Paul fretfully. " I simply can't think how you ever thought up this idea. It doesn't seem like you . . . Oh! " He looked at her swiftly. He could not see her face as she bent over the sink, quickly washing cups and saucers and piling them in the rack to drain. " It isn't your own idea, is it? " he said. " Didn't Brian suggest it? Didn't he put it into your head? "

" No," said Rachel flatly.

" Are you sure? "

" I'm quite sure."

" Because if he did, you might think over the fact that he's got a key to the cottage and can get in any time he likes."

" Only he doesn't much like."

" How do you know? "

" Because he says so." She was working faster and faster, flinging plates into the rack with reckless speed.

Paul frowned at the second glass that he had picked up. He knew that he was making a mess of things, antagonising her pointlessly, sowing trouble for the future. But something tense inside him, something under great pressure, prevented him sensibly leaving the matter there.

" It seems to me there's something distinctly strange about the fact that Brian apparently never went near the cottage yesterday, although he knew Miss Dalziel had come home," he said. " So I can't help wondering if perhaps he did go there, but for reasons of his own has seen fit not to mention it. His feelings about her may not have been exactly kindly, if he'd just heard she was going to turn him out without warning, and I shouldn't be at all surprised if he at least knows something about what happened to her."

Rachel did not answer at once. She did not flare up at him, as he had half-expected. She went on with the washing-up and Paul began to feel pleased that he had uttered his warning. What he did not notice was that she was trembling.

At last she said, " No one's suggested anything to me, unless it was that detective. He suggested to me I might have noticed something unusual when I took the milk round to the cottage—a noise, or a light, or a shadow, or something. And now, the more I think about it, the more I feel sure I did, though I can't think what it was. That's all."

But it was not all, by any means, and for that reason Rachel found it very hard to keep her voice down to that soft, level pitch. For of course it had been Brian who had suggested that Margot Dalziel might not have been as pleased at the marriage as Roderick had led Jane and the rest of them to believe. It had been Brian who had pointed out that Roderick was frightened of her and that she was someone of whom it was fairly easy to be frightened. A little Caesar, Brian had said.

Rachel's imagination had gone on from there. A little neurotic, possessive, outwitted Caesar, exhausted by unceasing hard work and the demands she made on herself, losing all control of herself and becoming crazy and cruel. . . .

Neither Paul nor Rachel slept well that night and next morning breakfast was late. The night had been noisy with a wind that had sprung up about midnight, and with rain lashing the windows. The house had been full of creaking and banging. Twice Paul had got up to try to wedge the window-frames in his room to stop them making a noise like machine-gun fire, but his wedges had not been effective and the rattling had pursued him, along with his worries, into short bouts of troubled dreaming. Now, instead of a sparkling, hushed, motionless world, there was a blustering wet one.

For some reason, Paul felt this to be an improvement. He felt as if some anxiety of the day before might turn out to have melted away in the night, and if this was irrational, at least it helped the three cups of strong coffee that he always needed at breakfast to make him feel able to face the day to come. He was grateful too to Jane and Roderick for being sound asleep still. There was no sound of anyone stirring yet in the spare bedroom.

But Rachel, as she sat facing her father in a nervy silence and watching the tossing of the bare branches of some chestnuts that she could see from the window, and the tumbling across the sky of ragged clouds, felt that the wildness of the weather was a new threat to her peace of mind. When some broken twigs clattered against the windowpane, she exclaimed as if she expected the glass to shatter. The ringing of the door-bell made her start from her chair as if the sound were some menacing effect of the gale.

The man at the door was the man whom she had seen in the road on Saturday evening, and whom she had sent to the barn to look for Miss Dalziel. Rachel knew him at once, although in several ways he was rather different from how she had remembered him. He was a good deal younger than she had imagined then, for his hair was not grey, as she had thought in the dusk, but unusually fair, and he had fair, almost invisible eyebrows above light grey eyes. He was tall and slender and stooped slightly. His face was composed and guarded, with only the slightest of family resemblances to the vivid face of his sister.

He spoke in the hurried, nervous voice that Rachel remembered.

" I'm sorry to call so early, but I've been to the barn and talked to Mr. Burden and he told me you might know where my nephew is. My nephew Roderick."

"Yes, he's here," said Rachel. "He and Jane spent the night here. Come in—I'll call them."

"Thank you," he said. "It seems you and Mr. Hardwicke have been immensely kind. There hasn't, I suppose, been any news of my sister?"

"None that I've heard," said Rachel. "I'm so sorry."

"I'm sorry you're being so troubled with the affairs of my family," he said.

Paul came out of the living-room and Rachel introduced them.

"I'm sorry to call so early," Neil Dalziel repeated. "I'm going on to see the police, but I thought if I could see Roderick first . . ."

"Of course, of course," said Paul. "Have you had breakfast?"

"Oh yes, thank you."

"A cup of coffee, then."

They went into the living-room and Rachel went upstairs to tell Roderick that his uncle had arrived. Jane's sleepy voice answered her, saying that they would both be down in just one minute.

When Rachel returned to the living-room, she found Neil Dalziel seated at the table, with a cup of coffee in front of him, which he was stirring rapidly and absent-mindedly, while he talked with the jerky loquacity of a shy, highly strung man.

"I'll have to go to the police this morning, of course," he said, "though I've very little to tell them. It's a long time since I've seen my sister. We both live in London, yet it must be—oh, two years since I saw her last. We quarrelled whenever we met, so it seemed best to avoid meeting. I remember, even when we were children, our relationship was a sort of running battle. My sister always had an extremely strong will, which she was determined to exercise entirely for my good, even when I didn't see things in the same light as she did. However, whenever anything serious happens, that kind of quarrelling shows up in all its ghastly triviality. It leaves behind a horrible sense of futility and guilt. Because she did mean well. Her intentions were always as good as they could possibly have been."

" At least you can comfort yourself you had a reconciliation," said Paul, " as I suppose you must have, since you came to see her on Saturday."

" Oh, but we hadn't," said Dalziel quickly, the teaspoon in his hand still swirling round and round in the cup before him. " Not at all. I came down here to tell her what I thought of her. It was nearly always the other way round, but just for once, I thought, I'd do it. I felt I couldn't let things go on as they were."

" Then we've misunderstood the situation," said Paul. " We thought you came down on Saturday to meet Jane and Roderick and discuss modernising that old barn for them to live in."

Dalziel gave a sharp shake of his head. " I hadn't agreed to do that. It's true she asked me to come down for that reason, and I agreed to come. I thought I'd got to, considering what she was planning. The thing had to be stopped, if it could be. But I hadn't any intention whatever of taking on a job for Margot. Actually I don't think I'd have done that in any circumstances, quite apart from my feeling about this particular project. As I said just now, when we met we quarrelled. It may have been much more my fault than I like to think, but that never made it any more enjoyable."

" I don't understand," said Paul uneasily. " Just what was Miss Dalziel planning that had to be stopped? "

" Keeping Roderick eternally under her thumb, as she'd tried with me," said Dalziel, with some suppressed excitement in his voice." He'd shown a little independence for once, getting married without consulting her. So it was time for her to let go and give the girl a chance— and give Roderick a chance too to grow into a responsible human being. Can't you see what would have happened if they'd settled down here? "

" They appear to have been very happy about the idea," said Paul.

" I don't doubt it," said Dalziel. " It wouldn't surprise me much if Roderick suggested it. But it would have been damned bad for him if you don't mind my saying so. He's never stuck to a job of work in his life and if he was given the chance now to slip into being Margot's caretaker and gardener and odd-job man about the house, like that chap Burden, it would just about finish him off."

His tone in speaking of Brian stung Rachel to anger.

" Why do you think that's what she planned, Mr. Dalziel? " she asked.

" It probably isn't," he said, " but it's what would have happened. And I thought I owed it to Roderick, or at least to the unfortunate girl who's married him, to try to stop it if I could."

" So if it was a failing of Miss Dalziel's to arrange other people's lives for them," said Rachel, " it's one that runs in the family."

He gave her a quick puzzled look, as if he had heard the note of resentment in her voice, but could imagine no possible reason for it.

" I've never thought of it like that, but you may be quite right, Miss Hardwicke," he said with the first smile that she had seen on his face. " I've always thought of myself as someone who didn't in the least want to push other people around, but only wanted exceedingly badly not to be pushed around myself. But perhaps that's how it always seems to oneself, whatever one's doing."

" Mr. Dalziel," said Paul, fidgeting on his chair, " I don't want you to misunderstand what I'm going to say to you. And first—you do realise, don't you, that the police are considering the possibility that your sister's been murdered? "

Dalziel seemed to become aware at last of the spoon in his hand and carefully put it down in his saucer.

" I realise it's a possibility they've got to consider now," he said.

" Yes. Well then," said Paul, " I don't want to give you the feeling that I'm warning you that what you say may be written down and used in evidence, but still, in the circumstances—well, you see what I mean, don't you? Actually to *exaggerate* the degree of your antagonism to your sister might make you some quite unnecessary trouble."

" What makes you think I'm exaggerating? " asked Dalziel.

Paul began to feel annoyed. He felt that the man was going farther than was decent.

" Oh, if you insist on sticking to it . . ."

Dalziel's cheeks flushed faintly. " I'm afraid it'll stick to me. Too many people know all about it for me to stand much chance of concealing it."

" You intend to tell the police about it? "

" Of course."

" You see, I don't like the idea of repeating what's been said to me privately in my home by someone who perhaps hasn't understood the seriousness of the situation," said Paul.

" Its seriousness," said Dalziel, standing up as Jane and Roderick came in, " is about the only part of it I do understand."

Jane and Roderick both showed signs of having dressed in a hurry. Roderick was in a shirt and flannels, without a jacket or tie and without having shaved. He was white-faced and his eyes looked over-large and over-bright. Jane was in jeans and a loose sweater, with her fair, wispy hair on end. There was a downy, sleepy, lost look about her, as if she had just crawled out of an egg. She gave the room a rather tremulous smile, but when Roderick, without any warmth in his voice, introduced Neil Dalziel to her, her smile grew radiant. She started to say how wonderful it was to meet another relation of Roderick's, but almost as soon as she began, Roderick cut across her with a tense sort of haste.

" Neil, now you're here, will you do something for me? " It sounded as if he felt that unless he hurried, some priceless opportunity might be lost for ever. " Will you tell Jane about that conversation you had with Margot on the telephone on Friday evening, when she told you about our getting married and asked you if you'd help her convert the barn for us? Will you tell her that Margot was really pleased? I've told Jane all about it myself, and I've discovered she doesn't believe me. I've discovered she's afraid Margot wasn't pleased at all and that I murdered her because of it. So will you please tell her what Margot said to you, word for word? "

CHAPTER VIII

" WORD FOR word," said Dalziel slowly, looking from Roderick to Jane, " is rather a tall order."

" Darling, darling," said Jane, clutching Roderick's hand, " you talk such awful nonsense. I keep telling you, that isn't what I meant at all. I'm absolutely sure Margot *thought* she was pleased about our marriage and that every single thing you've told me about it is true." She sat down at the table and turned her determined, brilliant smile on Rachel. " We're putting you to such an awful lot of trouble coming down so dreadfully late and everything. But we'll move out immediately after breakfast. We've decided there really isn't any reason at all why we shouldn't stay in the cottage."

" Neil," said Roderick, raising his voice, " do you mind doing what I asked you? "

Dalziel looked inquiringly at Paul, who made a little gesture, advising him to go ahead.

" Well then, to the best of my ability," said Dalziel,

" if not quite word for word. Margot rang me up on Friday evening and told me about your marriage. She sounded just as pleased about it as Roderick said. She was laughing and excited and she said wasn't it a joke that Roderick should have gone off and secretly married the one girl whom she'd been longing he'd realise existed."

" There, you see," said Jane to Roderick, as if it were really he who needed convincing. " Though as a matter of fact, I don't altogether understand why Margot's always been so wonderful to me, unless perhaps it's really my family she likes. You know, my mother being a J.P. and Margot writing all those things on juvenile delinquency and nicer prisons and so on. She may feel mother's the horse's mouth."

" Go on, Neil," said Roderick " There was more of it."

" Yes," said Dalziel, " she told me she wanted to do all she could for you both and that she had an old barn at the bottom of her garden which she thought could be converted into a very charming small house. She talked on a good while about that. She had all sorts of ideas about it. And she asked me if I would take charge of the job for her. I said . . ." He made the shortest of pauses as if he were changing his mind about what to tell them of his own feelings. " I said I'd come down here on Saturday afternoon and discuss the affair with her."

" How kind of you, how wonderfully kind! " cried Jane. " And of her. And of course the barn is wonderful too."

" With only the small disadvantage that there's someone living in it already," said Rachel.

" Brian? " said Jane. " Darling Brian." That seemed, for her, to dispose of his claims.

" Well, go on," said Roderick insistently to Dalziel.

" Isn't that the gist of things? " said Dalziel. " What have I left out? "

" Something quite important," said Roderick.

" Remember, I was there in the room with Margot when she was telephoning. I know what she said."

" If you mean that Margot and I argued a certain amount about the advisability of converting the barn and that I was against the idea . . ."

" I don't mean that," Roderick broke in excitedly. " You know I don't. Didn't she say to you, Neil, that if there was any hope I was going to settle down and behave like a reasonable human being, she'd get on and make her will. Isn't that so? "

" I believe it is, Roderick," said Dalziel.

" And she meant that she would leave what she had to me."

" So I understood."

" You did? You're sure? "

" Oh yes. I knew she'd always intended to do that, once she made up her mind to bother with making a will at all."

" But the fact is that meanwhile, if she'd died intestate, all she had would have gone to you, wouldn't it? "

The shadows under Dalziel's light-coloured eyes seemed suddenly to grow darker. He dropped his voice, as if in a precaution against letting it rise.

" I'm not really sure, Roderick. I'm not very well up in the laws about intestacy. I imagine you would have had your share, as the son of my brother."

" But if she'd ever made that will, you'd have lost everything—you knew that."

" I may have known it, but oddly enough, I don't remember thinking about it," said Dalziel.

" Yet only a day later, Margot—vanished."

Neil Dalziel said nothing. He stirred slightly, but it was only a faint relaxing of his muscles, as if he now knew where he was. But with that minute movement the atmosphere in the room seemed suddenly to change. Anything might be said now, anything might happen. There was naked enmity in Roderick's pale face.

But Neil Dalziel only gave a rather bleak smile and stood up.

"Well, as someone who seems to be rapidly developing into Suspect Number One," he said, " I think I ought to be getting along to see the police. I'll do my best to explain that point of yours to them, Roderick, unless by any chance you'd like to come with me and do it yourself."

Instead of answering, Roderick suddenly put his hands to his head and began to shake it from side to side. After a moment he started to mutter something about not having meant anything that he had been saying. His voice sounded close to tears.

At that moment Rachel heard with relief the clink of milk-bottles in the road and hurriedly escaped from the room.

She was just in time to catch the milkman, who had put a pint bottle down by the back door and was striding away, whistling.

She shouted after him. " Wait! I want another pint to-day. And look at that—just look! "

As he returned, she pointed furiously at the bottle and at the chipped cup with the broken handle on the ground beside it.

" Would it have been such an awful lot of trouble to put that cup over the top of the bottle? " she demanded. " Haven't I asked you to do it over and over again? And haven't you promised over and over again that you would?"

The man gave her a cocky, unrepentant smile.

" Well, Miss Hardwicke, I kind of get to thinking of something else and I forget like," he said. " But I won't do it again. Never. You can count on me."

" Oh, can I!" she said. " I can tell you, I'm going to make an unholy fuss with your boss if I find I can't."

" But the birds didn't get at it to-day, did they? No harm done, is there? "

"Only because I happened to be here, because I wanted to ask for an extra pint."

"It's the bluetits," he said, as if he felt that that successfully shifted the blame. He handed Rachel another bottle. "You only got to leave the bottle out a minute or two sometimes and they get it."

"They wouldn't if you'd put the cup on top of the bottle," said Rachel.

"Funny, now, bluetits," he said. "I like them. We got them in the garden at home. The missus puts bread out for them on the lawn."

"So do I," said Rachel. "I don't want them getting at my milk, however."

"Well, I'll remember, Miss Hardwicke. You can count on me. I'll never forget again," he promised glibly. "It's just that to-day I got things on my mind. Jim Gower's been at me this morning about a milk-bottle I left on Miss Dalziel's doorstep on Saturday. 'Did you leave one?' he said. 'Yes,' I said. 'When?' he said. 'The usual time,' I said. 'When would that be?' he said. 'Quarter past—half past eleven—thereabouts,' I said. 'And did the empty bottle get put out on the doorstep next day?' he said. 'Why,' I said, 'now that you come to mention it, I don't believe so,' I said. 'Are you sure?' he said. 'Are you so sure you'd swear to it in court?' he said. 'Yes,' I said, 'I'd swear to that in court.' Then he said, 'What about seeing it anywhere else, Bob? You seen that empty milk-bottle anywhere else?' And I said, 'No, Jim.' And he said, 'Bob,' he said, 'think about it, because that empty milk-bottle's important. It may be the crux of the matter.' And suddenly I remembered where I seen the bottle and I told him and that's on Mr. Burden's doorstep down at the old barn ... Well, good morning, Miss Hardwicke, and don't worry about your milk. The birds won't get at it again, never. You can count on me."

He strode away, whistling.

Rachel put the milk into the refrigerator and went slowly back to the living-room.

She found that Neil Dalziel was just leaving. He tried to say good-bye to her, but she looked blindly through him. As soon as he had gone, she went back to the kitchen, opened the refrigerator again and stared in the same blank way at the milk-bottles that she had just put into it. Two ordinary pint bottles, full of milk. Naturally they had nothing to tell her.

As she closed the refrigerator, she heard her father's step behind her. He came close to her and put an arm round her shoulders.

" What happened? " he asked, his voice low, in case he could be overheard from the living-room.

Without turning, she answered, " I'm wondering about something. How can a milkman tell one empty milk-bottle from another—if he *can* tell one empty milk-bottle from another? "

He drew her round to face him. " Don't put me off, my dear. I haven't seen a look like that on your face since . . . Oh, I don't know since when. Tell me what happened."

She put a hand to her face as if to brush away the look that he had seen. Her voice was quite calm. " I'm not putting you off. I really was wondering if that man can possibly tell his milk-bottles apart."

" I shouldn't think there's the slightest chance of it," said Paul. " What yarn has he been telling you? "

" Something I can't make sense of. He told me Gower had been at him this morning about the milk he left for Miss Dalziel on Saturday. Gower wanted to know if he'd found the empty bottle out on her doorstep yesterday. He said he hadn't, but he said he did find it on Brian's doorstep."

Paul did not mean to let his hand drop from her shoulder. It seemed simply to happen of itself when she spoke Brian's name. The next moment he found himself standing alone, with Rachel all of a sudden very busy at the other end of the kitchen, apparently checking stores in a cupboard.

With her back to him again, as calmly as ever, she went on, "And so I was wondering, you see, how he thinks he can tell that particular bottle from all his other bottles. How can he be sure the extra bottle wasn't one that Brian simply forgot to put out earlier in the week? I don't always put our own bottles out every single day. If one isn't empty, I keep it till next day."

Paul was listening to her, but he was also thinking about his helpless, stupid self-betrayal. With quiet horror, he realised that although he had never even imagined the possibility that Rachel could become hostile to him, that was what had happened, or half-happened. She might not yet be fully aware of the feeling, or she might at least be trying to resist it, but the ugly thing was there, waiting to be brought to very dangerous life by only one or two more blunders of the kind that he had just made.

Automatically he reached for the biscuit tin and helped himself to a ginger-nut.

"The man was talking nonsense," he said. "And you're quite right, of course. Even if there was one more bottle than usual on Brian's doorstep on Sunday, no one could be sure it was the same one that was left for Miss Dalziel on Saturday. It couldn't even be traced by finger-prints, because it would have gone into the sterilizer some-time yesterday."

"Yes—yes, of course!" said Rachel, with an eager-ness of response to him that reassured Paul to some extent, although at the same moment he felt a leaden pressure on his heart, which it took him a moment to recognise as the first painful stage of becoming resigned to the inevitable. "I hadn't thought about things like fingerprints. So the police won't necessarily believe him, will they?"

Slowly munching, Paul thought that a more important question was, whether or not she believed him herself.

" Going back to the question of why they're asking about that bottle," he said, " I'm not sure if I mentioned to you that they couldn't find it in the cottage, full or empty, and that's certainly rather strange."

" Anyway, I can't see Brian helping himself to it, and if he didn't, I don't see how it could have turned up on his doorstep," said Rachel, and felt so cheered by this reasoning that she suddenly carolled a few bars of song, and picking up a tray, went back to the living-room to clear the breakfast.

Paul took three more ginger-nuts out of the tin and went to his study, but after only a few minutes he gave up the idea of trying to work on his book and decided instead to go for a walk. He went downstairs again, put on his coat and cap and let himself out. The wind immediately snatched at his cap, tore it from him and carried it straight into a hawthorn bush. Swearing, he went after it, but by the time that he had managed to extricate it from the thorns, his hands were scratched and his white hair was in elf locks. Putting the cap in a pocket, he went striding off down the road, bareheaded.

The incident had released his bad temper and he scowled and muttered as he walked through the blustery weather. The feeling of resignation was one with which he was not very familiar and he found it extremely distressing. It felt, he found, almost the same as defeat and he did not want to believe yet that he had been finally defeated in protecting Rachel from herself.

" Yet I may be wrong—I'm capable of being wrong—anyone can be wrong," he said, his lips moving animatedly, although no sound came from them. " But I'll be hanged if I believe I am. This business of sitting around in barns, writing books nobody's ever going to hear of . . . Oh well, I may be wrong about that too. I admit it freely. He may be the genius of the century—only I'll be hanged if I believe that either! No, no, he's not the right man for her. About that I'm absolutely sure I'm right. . . ."

He came to a sudden standstill. A voice inside his

head, which he rarely heard nowadays, had just said to him distinctly, " You bloody fool, you're always so damned sure you're right! "

It was his wife's voice, or at least an echo of it, the echo that still occasionally came, after fifteen years, always when he was least prepared for it, sometimes tender and reassuring, but sometimes, as it had just been, softly ferocious.

Paul gave a slight shudder and walked on.

He and Mary had always quarrelled a great deal. Their relationship had been one of heights and depths, both of which, at this distance, were difficult to remember or quite to believe in. The long calm of his relationship with Rachel had made that other seem like the fantasy of a somewhat unbalanced imagination. Was it possible that he had once been a person who had said, had done, some of the violent things which it seemed to him he remembered that he had, while at the same time loving with passion a person who had said and done as bad, or worse, to him?

He knew for a fact that he had been such a person and also that between the explosions there had been periods of sweetness which were now even harder to recall than the storms because of the pain stirred by their memory. But he was a very different sort of man now. He liked peace. He liked to feel tolerably certain that in half an hour's time he would be experiencing neither some unpredictable heaven nor bewildering hell, but just comfortably doing what he had mapped out for himself.

" All right, all right," he said wildly to his memory of Mary, waving an arm as he walked. " I'm wrong about everything—I'm always the one who's wrong—I admit it freely, I admit it freely."

He was really admitting more than that he could be wrong. He was admitting that Rachel had a right to be wrong in her own way too, without interference from him. He was admitting, further, that since she was undoubtedly determined to be wrong about Brian Burden, there was nothing to be gained by interference but pain and loss, a loss far worse than the mere loss of her dear company, which of course her marriage at any time would mean.

So there you were, he thought. Wasn't that resignation, after all? Wasn't that admitting defeat with a pretty good grace, while even beginning to consider what, if anything, he could do to help her? At just that moment, however, it seemed clear to him that nothing would be quite so helpful all round as a drink, and as he had just reached the Waggoners, he turned in at the door.

There was only one other man in the bar when Paul entered. He was sitting close to the oil stove, which was the only heating that Mrs. Dunn, the licensee of the small pub, allowed her customers in the morning. The man looked round as Paul came in and Paul saw that it was Inspector Creed.

They nodded to one another, but Mrs. Dunn was in the middle of telling Creed who had murdered Miss Dalziel and how and why, so neither he nor Paul ventured to speak to each other. She was a majestic woman, with a moon face resting on several chins on a horizontal bosom, who dominated any conversation in which she condescended to join and was offended at interruption.

It stood to reason, didn't it, Mrs. Dunn was saying, a thing like that couldn't be coincidence. Anyone hereabouts would tell Creed the same. They all knew what had happened without having to be told. She herself had known it from the first and she knew too just what she'd do about it if she was given the chance, because you couldn't have this state of affairs going on, not with hardly a woman in the place feeling safe. She didn't feel safe herself, all alone here half the day, and no one even within call, if that boy was to show up here and cut her throat and empty the till. And of course it was him, because they'd all been expecting trouble anyway, as soon as they knew he was home, so it stood to reason, didn't it?

She was back to where she had been when Paul came

in and would certainly have continued round the circle again if a kettle had not started to whistle in her kitchen. Excusing herself, she made a stately exit.

Paul turned to Creed with a wry smile. " So they've settled on young Applin."

" Without exception," said Creed. " It was murder, young Applin did it and they were all expecting it, or something like it. And the mere fact that we've been checking up on him has settled his hash. And to a man— or rather, to a woman—they know what they'd do with him if they had the chance."

Paul studied Creed's face, with the skin that seemed to fit too tightly over the bones behind it and the reserved, defensive gaze.

" You don't sound so convinced yourself," said Paul.

"I'm trained to pay some attention to facts," said Creed sombrely, " even when it's annoying to have to believe in them. The main fact about Applin at the moment is that he can account for his time for the whole of Saturday. . . ."

He stopped, turning his head swiftly to the door. It was opening, but strangely slowly and noiselessly, almost as if it had come open of itself, and nothing came in but a strong, cold gust of the wind that made the flame of the oil stove flicker.

Then as Paul started towards the door to shut it again, there was a sound of whispering voices outside, a small, dirty hand grasped the edge of the door and pushed it a little further open and Bernice Applin sidled in.

CHAPTER IX

SHE WORE her ragged, bright red coat that left inches of her thin wrists sticking out from the cuffs. Her hair was in a wind-blown tangle. Her cheeks were bright as berries.

Strolling forward to the bar, she gave Paul one of her ingratiating smiles and taking two half-crowns out of her pocket, rapped with them on the bar. It was only then, as Mrs. Dunn came sailing haughtily in, drawn by the sound of the coins on the counter, that Bernice saw Creed.

It was a moment of some embarrassment for everybody, for not only had Creed spent a good deal of the morning in her home, questioning her brother and parents, so that there was no possibility of either his or her pretending that he was not a policeman, but there could be no doubt of the fact that Bernice was under fourteen and had no business to be on licensed premises.

Mrs. Dunn coped with the situation by giving Bernice a freezing look of surprise, as if she had never seen her there before, and ordered her out, while Creed tactfully peered with profound concentration into his glass until Bernice was safely outside again and the door had been shut on the burst of giggles that greeted her.

" Well, did you ever? " said Mrs. Dunn. " Coming in as if she owned the place. Whatever will those children get up to next? It's like I told you, Mr. Creed—" She folded her thick arms on the bar and gave him a stern glare, as if it had been he who had encouraged the child to break the law. " The mother's no good and the father's worse and in my opinion they're the ones who ought to be put in gaol, not just that Kevin. It's no good being soft with that sort or looking the other way to save yourselves trouble. If you do, trouble is what you'll get, bad trouble. It stands to reason. . . ."

Rumbling on indignantly, she went back to her tea.

" There's gratitude for you," said Creed. " What was the child after? Buying her father's cigarettes for him? "

" Probably," said Paul.

" And now she'll have to go all the way to the village shop? "

" I suppose so."

" Seems a silly business, doesn't it? Let's hope the exercise will do her good."

" I should think exercise is about the one thing she doesn't go short of," said Paul. He drank some of his beer. " You were just telling me what Kevin was doing on Saturday morning."

" Oh yes," said Creed. " Well, it happens that on Saturday morning Kevin rode off on his motorbike to see his old employer, a man called Browder, a market gardener, to see if he could have his job back. And Browder agreed to take him on, starting to-day. There's no question at all that about the time that bottle of milk disappeared from Miss Dalziel's doorstep, Kevin was four miles away, with Browder. And he can account for the rest of the day too. After seeing Browder, he rode on into Fallford, where he picked up with two old friends and the three of them settled down to get drunk in the White Lion. Then they went off to the pictures to sleep it off, and then to a snack bar for fish and chips. It's quite easy to check his trail all the way, because he and his friends made themselves troublesome enough to be remembered. He got home about eight, so his mother says, went straight to bed and didn't stir till morning."

" I'm afraid that what his mother says isn't something that you can entirely rely on," said Paul.

Creed gave his tight-lipped smile. " Even so, if it's true that Miss Dalziel's brother didn't find her at home and couldn't get into the house when he arrived there around half past five, it doesn't much matter what Applin did after eight, does it? "

" And he couldn't have taken the milk-bottle? "

" Definitely not." Creed's voice was flatter than usual, as he remembered that moment of inspiration yesterday, when he would have staked his reputation on his certainty that Kevin had taken the milk and murdered Margot Dalziel.

" About that milk-bottle," said Paul, " is it true that it turned up on Mr. Burden's doorstep? "

" According to the milkman, an extra bottle did turn up there on Sunday morning," said Creed, " but naturally there's no way of proving it was the bottle he left for Miss Dalziel on Saturday."

Paul finished his drink, and feeling that he had now a piece of good news to take home to Rachel, and that that made his home seem a more attractive place than it had an hour ago, he began to button his coat.

" All the same," Creed went on, " it seems Mr. Burden is pretty consistent about washing his bottles before he puts them out, and this bottle hadn't been washed, and he's pretty regular too about putting them out every day, so it isn't often there's more than the one there."

" Oh? " said Paul. " Oh, I see. Yes. Well . . ." Frowning and forgetting to say good morning, he let himself out into the road.

As if she had been waiting for him, Bernice instantly pounced on him, holding out her two half-crowns.

" Oh, Mr. Hardwicke, please! " she cried. " Please will you go in and buy my dad's cigarettes for me? Twenty Senior Service he likes. I've got the kids with me and they're tired, poor little things, and it's too far to the shop for Loraine without the pram and my dad'll take the skin off me if I go back without his cigarettes. Oh, please, Mr. Hardwicke! "

" Loraine? " said Paul, looking down the road to where the two younger children were dubiously watching Bernice treating with the enemy.

" That's right," said Bernice. " Isn't it a pretty name? "

" Charming," said Paul. " And what's the other one? "

" She's Myrna."

" Well, your parents at least try to give you a good start in life," he said.

She beamed at him, pressing her two half-crowns into his hand. " Oh, thank you, Mr. Hardwicke, thank you so much, you're so kind," she said with the exaggerated primness that she sometimes assumed. " Mum always says so. ' Mr. Hardwicke's so kind and good,' she says."

" Funny," said Paul, as he turned back into the Waggoners to buy the cigarettes, " somehow they don't really sound like her adjectives."

When he came out again and gave the packet to Bernice, she thrust it into a pocket of her red coat, but kept the change clutched in her fist. Then for once, as Paul started homeward, she stayed at his side instead of running away from him and started to chat about the difficulties of her life, which would not be lessened, Paul was given to understand, if Mrs. Dunn were to stick to her absurd attitude of refusing to serve Bernice just because she was too young. From some distance ahead the two younger children looked back at this with scared suspicion and suddenly decided to run home without waiting for her.

As they took to their heels, Bernice shouted after them, but they took no notice and in a moment had vanished round the corner into the lane.

" There, look at that! " she said. " They're getting so they won't do a thing I tell them. Like the day I had to go and fetch them out of Miss Dalziel's garden and you come in and caught us."

" Oh, then it wasn't you who took them into the garden? " said Paul.

Bernice, who never noticed sarcasm, shook her head scornfully, setting her thick hair swinging. " ' Look,' I said to them, ' just you look at the trouble you got me into, taking care of you,' I said. 'Don't you never run off again like that,' I said, ' or I'll pin your ears back.

And don't you never touch nothing of the lady's, cos I won't get you out of trouble next time, just you remember that,' I said. But they don't listen to me, Mr. Hardwicke." She sighed. " They're quite out of my control, that's what they are, little bastards."

Paul wondered what it felt like to grow up under the threat of the unspeakable tortures which, according to Bernice, were commonly practised in the Applin family. Their ears were to be pinned back, their skin was to be taken off them, they were to have the living daylights knocked out of them, for the smallest offence. It was really more than medieval. And unfortunately entirely ineffective.

" If only I could persuade you to try the power of example . . ." he began.

But that was enough to make Bernice decide that she had had enough of Paul, and she suddenly started to shriek with ear-splitting power, " Myrna! Loraine! Myrna! Loraine! "

At the same time she started to run. The sound of her shrill shouting came back to Paul on the gusty wind as she vanished after the other two into the lane.

Paul went on homewards, thinking that if he had ever met a human being who seemed to have been doomed at birth, and through no particular fault of her own, it was Bernice. She had some good qualities, loyalty and affection and something that at a pinch you could call imagination, but these were about as little use to her in withstanding the influences of her deplorable environment as that ragged red coat of hers must be in keeping out the winter's cold.

Not that she had seemed to be suffering from the cold this morning. Her cheeks had been brilliant and her eyes sparkling. Whatever you felt like saying against the parents, the children always looked healthy. Healthy and in their way so beautiful. Paul shook his head, feeling an irritable depression growing in him. Then for an instant the bright, brutal face of young Kevin swam before him, and his thoughts went sharply back to Margot Dalziel.

If Kevin was out of it, what could have happened to the poor woman? *If* Kevin was out of it. . . .

Passing the end of the lane, Paul noticed a black car parked in it, thought for a moment that it was a police car and then that probably it was Neil Dalziel's. Going on past the thatched cottage, he just missed meeting Rachel in the road. She was taking Jane her bedroom slippers, which had been left behind when Jane and Roderick, soon after Paul had gone out, had insisted on packing and returning to the cottage, saying that they could not possibly impose on the Hardwickes any longer.

Rachel had been at Miss Dalziel's gate when Bernice's banshee cry, as she ran after her sisters, reached her from the lane. Rachel did not hear the words, but only a meaningless howl, which sounded as if the wind had suddenly taken on the quality of a human voice, and although it was broad daylight, her flesh crept. The wailing of a banshee meant that someone was going to die, didn't it? Or was it that someone had died? It was a bad thing to hear, anyway, even if you had been carefully educated not to be superstitious.

She walked up the path to the cottage, seeing smoke coming from its chimney. The smoke was flattened by the wind into a low, ragged cloud. Jane and Roderick, she thought, had wasted no time about lighting a fire in the sitting-room, needing, she supposed, something to take the feeling of death and disaster out of the place. She wondered if they had tidied up the room yet, or if everything was still as it had been, with the table overturned, the broken decanter on the floor, the stain on the rug, the ashes in the fireplace.

Suddenly she stood still, staring up at the chimney.

Ashes in the fireplace, she thought. A fire. Someone had lit a fire on Saturday. Yet there had been no smoke coming from the chimney when she had come over with the bottle of milk, and none all the afternoon, while she had been in the garden, raking up the fallen leaves. And that was strange. A fire without smoke. Or else a fire lit far earlier, or far later, than they had all been reckoning.

She walked on up the path. A moment later, as she passed the sitting-room windows, she became more sure than ever that if the fire in the great old fireplace had been alight when she came on Saturday morning, she would have noticed it, for the windows were so small and the walls so thick that the fire in the room now showed up as brightly as if it were burning in a cave. It lit up the whole room with its cheerful flickering. But on Saturday morning the windows had been blank and dark.

Rachel did not know what this meant, but realised that after all she had managed to remember something strange about her visit that day to tell Inspector Creed. She went on to the door and knocked.

It was opened after a moment by Jane, who said in surprise, " Oh! . . . Oh, I thought you were Roderick. He's gone to the village to buy us some groceries. Do come in. Come into the kitchen, if you don't mind, because I'm just trying to arrange some flowers."

" I only came to bring these," said Rachel, holding out the slippers. " I won't stay."

" Did I leave them behind? " said Jane. " Oh dear, I'm so sorry. The trouble we give you! But do please come in. You could tell me about these flowers, because I don't seem to be very good at them. And—and it would be much nicer than being alone in this place. It's doing awfully queer things to me. I keep getting an almost irresistible impulse to ring up my mother. Yet there's almost nothing I should hate more than to have her come tearing over and taking charge of everybody. Did you hear a ghastly scream just now? "

She had thrust her arm through Rachel's and was eagerly holding her in the doorway.

" Yes, I think it was just one of the Applin children," said Rachel, yielding and going in.

" You did hear it then? " said Jane. " That makes me feel much better. I was beginning to feel horribly afraid I'd imagined it and I was getting ready to start screaming myself. Now come along and tell me about my flower arrangement. Isn't that a horrible phrase? There's hardly anything to choose between it and floral tributes. And naturally I haven't any flowers, but only some bits and pieces of greenery, but the police took those roses of Margot's away, and the vase too for some reason, and I felt I simply had to put something in their place. There's something so horrible about that room still. . . ."

Chattering fast, as if she felt that this would make it impossible for Rachel to change her mind and leave her alone in the cottage, Jane took her to the kitchen.

The draining boards were littered with pieces of yew, holly and privet, and a few branches had been stuck in a stiff bunch into an earthenware jug that stood on the table.

" You see—it's a mess," said Jane. " I expect you're one of those wonderful people who could take about three of those pieces and add a cauliflower or something and make it look just like something out of a magazine. But if I put in only three pieces they all fall out. Oh well, it doesn't really matter. I only did it at all to have something to do while Roderick was gone. We had such an absurd quarrel this morning and what I really want to do is sit down and cry, only I've sworn to myself I won't. But I swore to myself too I wouldn't ever quarrel with Roderick, because if I do, I might just as well have stayed at home, where they quarrel all the time."

She wrenched a piece of privet out of the jug, stood back and looked mournfully at what remained.

" I hate this stuff," she said, throwing the privet into the sink, " but I thought perhaps I could be clever with it somehow. But I'm not clever and that's all there is to it. I wasn't being clever telling Roderick he oughtn't to have spoken to poor Neil like that about Margot's will. . . . Well, he oughtn't to have, do you think? But there wasn't any point in saying anything about it, because he only started saying that he just wanted to convince me that he hadn't murdered Margot, and so I started saying I never thought for a moment that he had and that as a matter of fact I thought she was probably going to walk in alive any moment now, and then Roderick started clutching his head and saying I was mad, and then he rushed off to buy those groceries. Did you ever hear anything so ridiculous?"

Rachel had sat down and put her elbows on the table. She looked up curiously at Jane's thin, anxious, childish face.

"Do you really believe she's alive," she asked, "or do you mean that it was saying that that was so ridiculous?"

"I'm sure she's alive," said Jane. She gave a sigh and picked up the vase. "I shan't make this any better however long I mess about with it. Come along, let's go through to the other room. There's a fire there."

"Wait a minute," said Rachel. "Why do you think she's alive, Jane?"

Jane frowned slightly, as if she could not quite remember why she had thought it.

"It's something to do with that room," she said uncertainly. "Last night I started wondering if there'd been a real struggle there at all. I'm not sure why. Anyway, I told Roderick, and that was the beginning of the trouble, because he went sarcastic and asked me if I thought it was poltergeists. And I laughed and said no, of course not, although, as a matter of fact, I don't laugh at things like that. I was just wondering, I said, if just possibly Margot had done it all herself. And Roderick thought I meant she'd done it in revenge on us for getting married and that I didn't believe she'd been as pleased about it as he'd told me and that I thought he'd—he'd lost his head at the things she'd said to him about it and murdered her, or something."

"And didn't you mean that—the revenge part?" said

Rachel, startled at hearing something so like the theory
that she herself had been playing with the evening before,
the theory that had grown out of her talk with Brian.

" No, of course not," said Jane. " I was absolutely
sure she'd be pleased about the marriage. But I did start
thinking that hearing we'd gone and done it secretly like
that might have been rather a shock to her. But she's
such a nice person, you see, she'd have leant over backwards not to show it. Then she might have come down
here. . . ."

" Yes? " said Rachel.

" Well, suppose she came down here and she was tired
from all that travelling, and rather worked up because of
us—and then suppose the person she was expecting didn't
come."

" *Didn't* come? " said Rachel. " I thought he's the
one who's supposed to have done it."

" But just suppose he didn't come," said Jane, " and
suppose she was sitting there, feeling upset about that too,
and awfully tired, and so she thought she'd have a drink
or two and then perhaps another couple."

Rachel shook her head. " I can't imagine Miss
Dalziel a solitary drinker, but go on," she said.

" Quite unexpected people are solitary drinkers sometimes," said Jane. " It wouldn't have to mean it was a
habit with her."

" I see. Well? "

" Well then, suppose she just let herself go after a
bit. . . . I mean, raged and shouted and started throwing
things about, threw over the table, smashed the decanter,
then slipped on the rug and hit her head hard on something and knocked herself out."

" Miss Dalziel? " said Rachel incredulously.

Jane nodded earnestly. " I honestly think it's the
likeliest explanation."

" But what happened to her then? "

" Oh, then the man she was expecting did turn up, of
course, and saw the state she was in, with her nose bleeding

on the rug and the room a shambles, and picked her up and carried her out to his car and drove home, wherever that is—and that's where they are now and much too interested in each other to think of us or take any notice of the papers and they're probably going to live happily ever after."

Rachel stood up. She said sadly, " He sounds a nice sort of man. Now I must go home, Jane."

" You don't believe any of it, do you? " said Jane, looking at her over the jugful of yew and holly. " But it would be nice to believe it, wouldn't it? "

" Very nice," said Rachel.

" Then why don't you try? "

" Because it's too nice."

" Well, I don't see what's wrong with believing something nice instead of something quite horribly nasty, when in fact you haven't the slightest idea what really happened." Jane turned to the door. " You haven't really got to go yet, have you? Can't you wait till Roderick gets back? "

She went ahead of Rachel to the door of the sitting-room, pushed it open and went down the two steps into the room.

There she stood still. The jug of greenery slipped from her hands to the floor with a crash. She screamed. Just before the door swung shut behind her in Rachel's face, Rachel had a glimpse of a figure inside the room moving swiftly forward.

CHAPTER X

RACHEL PUSHED at the door. It opened and she saw Jane and Neil Dalziel facing one another, with the jug and the bunch of evergreens on the floor between them.

" I'm sorry—I'm so sorry I scared you, Jane," Dalziel was saying, his face red with embarrassment. He had a book in his hands, one of the finely bound old books from the book-case. He gesticulated with it. " I didn't know you were here. I thought you were still at the Hardwickes'."

" You didn't scare me, you just startled me," Jane said shakily. " I suppose you came in while I was out, picking these things in the garden." She stooped over the wreck of her unlucky flower arrangement. " At least the jug didn't break. How did you get in? Have you a key? "

" No, but the door wasn't locked," he said. " Seeing the fire, I realised there'd been someone around, but I thought it was probably Margot's Mrs. Brooke. I didn't think of your being here. Where's Roderick? "

" He went to the village to buy us some things to eat," said Jane. She picked up the jug and the leaves. " Now I'd better do these over again, I suppose, and wipe up the mess. The police took away Margot's roses, for some reason, and the room somehow looks awful without anything, though I've tried to do some tidying up."

She turned and went out to the kitchen again.

Instead of leaving, as she had intended a minute or two before, Rachel went into the sitting-room. Most of the signs of disorder had gone, but because the police had removed the rug with the stain on it as well as the roses, the room had a bleak, uninhabited look.

" You knew we were here, didn't you? " she said. " You must have heard our voices in the kitchen."

Dalziel turned to the book-case, replacing the book that he was holding. "Well, yes," he said.

"Why weren't we supposed to know that?"

He turned to look at her with the searching, rather puzzled stare with which he had regarded her before, as if he could not decide where she fitted into the picture.

"For no very good reason," he said. "I apologise."

She gave a slight shake of her head.

"Ah well," he said, as if he were sorry that his answer did not satisfy her, since he could do no better. Turning back to the book-case, he reached for another book, opened it and idly turned the pages.

"Have you seen the police yet?" Rachel asked.

"Only Sergeant Gower," he said. "The inspector wasn't there, so I'm seeing him later."

"Haven't they any news at all?"

"No, and there seemed to be nothing much I could do, so I came here to have a look round. I imagine Jane was out in the garden, as she suggested, when I got here, because no one answered when I knocked, but the door was unlocked, so I came in."

"Then you heard me arrive and you heard us talking, and I suppose you listened to us. Is that what you don't want to admit?"

He came towards her as she stood by the fire. "Well, Jane had a rather interesting theory about Margot, hadn't she? I wanted to hear it all. But I also wanted to finish something I was doing in here before she came in and caught me. Not that it would really have mattered if she'd caught me, but there are times when one likes to keep a half-formed idea to oneself."

"And did you finish it?"

He hesitated, looking down at the book in his hands. His taut, pale face looked haggard.

"I think so. Now tell me, what did you think of Jane's theory?"

"Didn't you hear me saying that I didn't think much of it?"

"You didn't say it. Jane said it for you. You rather carefully avoided giving an opinion."

"Perhaps I did. That was mainly not to crush Jane's hopes—her hopes that Miss Dalziel's alive. Yet I had an idea something like it myself last night. . . ."

As soon as she had said that, Rachel wished that she had not, because she had convinced herself by now that the idea had been quite absurd and also that Brian must have known that it was absurd when he planted its seed in her brain. Unless, of course, she had misunderstood him. But at least he had managed to confuse her picture of Margot Dalziel, and with it her picture of himself. The uncertainty that now filled Rachel's mind about them both was something that she did not feel like discussing with anyone.

She did not have to discuss it with Neil Dalziel because Jane, returning with her rearranged vase and a mop to dry up the water that had been spilled on the floor, had heard Rachel saying something about hopes that Miss Dalziel was alive. Assuming that Rachel had been telling Dalziel of her theory, she said to him seriously, " I do want you to understand I never meant Margot was actually *upset* about Roderick getting married. I never meant she was against it. Roderick would have told me if she was. Anyway, you know yourself she wasn't, from the things she said to you on the telephone. I only meant that it cost her more to give him up than she wanted him to realise."

" So she took to the bottle? " It was not said mockingly. He seemed to be considering the idea quite soberly.

" Only when this man she was expecting didn't turn up," said Jane, putting the vase down on the little writing table beside the window, where the vase of roses had stood before.

" Have you any suspicion who he was, Jane? " asked Dalziel.

" No," she said.

" Yet you knew her pretty well."

" I suppose so."

" And you were fond of her."

" I loved her," said Jane.

" So don't you think, if there'd been such a man, you'd have known about him? "

" Oh, not necessarily," she said. " Margot very seldom talked about personal things. It wasn't that she was secretive, it was just that she didn't think them interesting. She talked about her job and politics and celebrities she'd met and so on."

He gave a dry laugh. " That's a telling little portrait of her . . . What? " He wheeled round, startled, because from the doorway Roderick had just shouted his name at him.

" That book you're holding, Neil—what the hell d'you think you're doing with it? " Roderick demanded. His face was remarkably white.

Dalziel did not answer. Returning to the book-case, he put the book back on its shelf.

Roderick came down the two steps into the room, still holding the basket full of groceries that he had been to fetch. With his voice shaking uncontrollably, he said, " You always wanted Margot's books, didn't you? You always thought grandfather should have left them to you, not to her. I don't suppose you'd really have grudged me anything else of hers, if she'd lived to make that will she talked about, but you couldn't bear the idea of those books coming to me."

" I came," said Dalziel, " because they're probably the most valuable things Margot possessed and it occurred to me it might be a good idea to find out if any of them were missing."

" Why should any of them be missing? " Roderick asked.

" Don't valuable things quite often go missing?" said Dalziel.

" If there's a thief around, yes."

They looked at one another through a moment of

angry silence. Then Roderick gave an ugly little smile. "Why don't you say what you mean, Neil—that you came to see if I'd been stealing Margot's books?"

"It doesn't have to be you, Roderick."

"Who else could it be?"

"There's Burden."

"Why Burden? Why not yourself, Neil?"

"I haven't a key to this cottage," said Dalziel.

"And Brian has. And so have I. But would it be so difficult to get in here without a key?"

"Perhaps not, but Sergeant Gower told me there were no signs of breaking in."

"I see. You've worked it all out quite carefully. Some books have been stolen—that's what you're going to tell them. And it'll somehow become very clear that you couldn't have taken them. And then in the end you'll get them all."

There was another taut silence in the room.

Then Dalziel said dully, "Isn't it a strange thing, Roderick, I never realised till this morning how much you hated me?"

"I never did hate you till this morning," Roderick said.

With a thin little cry, Jane clutched at Roderick's arm. "Don't *say* things like that—don't! Hate's horrible."

"Don't worry, Jane," said Dalziel. "Nobody hates you."

"But I hate—I hate being *near* hatred!" she wailed.

"And now why don't you go?" said Roderick to Dalziel. "Jane and I are staying here and we'd like to be alone for a change. We'd like it very much."

Jane gave a gasp of shame and because of the agony in her great eyes, Rachel managed a rather stiff smile and said, "Oh, in your place I'd feel the same. And in any case I didn't mean to stay so long. Don't worry."

Roderick's face went scarlet. "I didn't mean—oh God, I'm sorry! I didn't mean you, Rachel. This is just family stuff. It—it doesn't mean anything. It'll blow over. Please don't go."

But Rachel said that she had come only to bring Jane her slippers and had never meant to come in at all. As she went on her way, Neil Dalziel followed her.

In the garden the wind buffeted her cheeks, tore at her hair and fastened a chill grip on her throat. She turned up the collar of her coat and began to hurry, wanting to get away as quickly as she could both from the cottage and from the man who now stayed at her side, and who reached the gate just before her and put his hand on it, looking as if he were about to open it for her, but in fact preventing her from opening it herself.

" Miss Hardwicke, please—can we talk for a moment?" he said.

She thought of his suspicion of Brian and wanted to answer that she had no time, but before she had made up her mind to say that, he went on, " I'd like to know, do you know Brian Burden well? "

Rachel felt her features harden with animosity. " Fairly well," she said.

She was wondering how he had come to the cottage, because his car was neither in the drive, nor in the road, and it was Roderick's car that she could see through the half-open door of the garage.

" I met him for the first time this morning," said Dalziel, as if this were the beginning of something that he wanted to say. But then he gave a slight shrug and began to open the gate. " Oh well, I suppose things will sort themselves out somehow."

Rachel stayed where she was. " Those books," she said. " Some of them are missing, aren't they? "

" I think so," he said.

" And you were going to ask me if I thought Brian could have taken them? "

" I was going to—yes. But your face told me what your answer was going to be and that probably you were going to hate me if I asked you. And I don't believe I like hatred any more than poor Jane does."

He gave an unhappy smile and Rachel realised that he was far more agitated and far more distressed than she had recognised in the cottage.

" Are they very valuable, the missing ones? " she asked.

" Not enormously," he said. " Perhaps about two hundred pounds altogether, unless there are more gone than I think. I hadn't much time to look, before Jane came in, but I couldn't find either Newton's *Optical Lectures* or his *Method of Fluxion and Infinite Series*. They're both first editions of the first English translations from the Latin, published around 1730, and I'd guess they're worth about a hundred pounds each. But there could be others missing as well."

" If any are missing at all," said Rachel. " If you'd so little time, couldn't you have overlooked those two? "

" Just possibly."

" And even if they aren't there, it doesn't mean they've been stolen. Miss Dalziel might have lent them to someone, or they may have needed attention of some sort, or perhaps she sold them."

" Yes, I know. But you see . . ." He was swinging the gate to and fro and it was making a faint, creaking, protesting note under his hand. " Margot's disappearance makes one distrust the obvious explanations of the small unusual things. And for those books, which she treasured very much, not to be there, is at least unusual."

" You're really afraid Roderick stole them, aren't you? "

He went on swinging the gate and the noise of it got so on Rachel's nerves that suddenly she grasped the top bar of it and slammed it shut. Dalziel smiled.

" I'm sorry. The way Roderick's behaving at the moment has got badly under my skin and I don't quite know what I'm doing. And I don't know what I think about him. We used to get on very well when he was a child and though I don't often see him now, I suppose I've always taken for granted that he was quite attached to me. But he's fighting his private war against the world, isn't he? And I seem to belong to the enemy."

" Isn't this war really against your sister? "

He answered reluctantly, " It must be, I suppose. And I suppose I could add that I saw it coming and that it was mainly her own fault. Having been through it with her myself, I know the mixture of love and admiration and furious resentment that she can inspire in a boy—or a man, rather, a young man who's got tired of being a boy. But I oughtn't to be talking like this. Your father warned me not to exaggerate my antagonism to Margot and I denied that there was any exaggeration about it, but there is, of course. Exaggeration and bravado, because even at my age I've never managed to come to terms with the problems she created."

The smile that went with that was sardonic, but gentler than before.

" I'm rather attracted by Jane's theory," he went on. " It gives me a quite new view of Margot—one I like a good deal better than the old one. It makes her rather pathetic and quite human. I think I'd begin to like her again if there were anything in it."

" But you don't think there is," said Rachel.

" Do you? "

" I hardly know her. We've only lived here a few months."

" Ah, I didn't realise that." He seemed to think that over, as if to see if it affected the situation. " No, I can't manage to believe in it," he said. " I wish I could. But for one thing, there'd still be the riddle of where she's got to now."

" What about the man who came and took her away, the one who brought her the roses—or for whom she bought them? He was part of the theory."

" I'll start to believe in him when we find someone who's seen him. Margot liked men, she enjoyed their company, but she was about as unpassionate as a woman can be."

" I wonder how much a brother would really know about that."

For an instant his light grey eyes concentrated on Rachel's, then he shrugged his shoulders. " Well, perhaps not much. Perhaps he does exist. Again, I'd be very glad if he did. If Margot's self-sufficiency turned out not to be real, I'd be far less scared of her."

" The only person who seems not to be in the least scared of her," said Rachel, " is Jane, which is curious, because she seems such a frightened creature."

" Perhaps then, she doesn't mind being dependent on Margot. Perhaps she finds such strength very reassuring."

" But somebody must have come to the cottage that day," said Rachel. " Your sister was expecting somebody."

" Because of the roses and the drinks? "

" Yes, and the fire . . ." She stopped. She had almost told him what she had remembered about the fire and the smoke on Saturday afternoon. But she had decided a little while ago not to tell anyone about it until she had discussed it with her father. " I suppose she might have lit the fire just for herself," she said, " and perhaps even bought the roses for herself. But she wouldn't have brought out two sherry glasses for herself."

" So of course she expected somebody, or arrived with somebody, or somebody was waiting for her."

" *Waiting*. . . ? "

" Why not? " he said. " Suppose she'd found Burden in the cottage, mightn't she have offered him a drink, even if their relationship didn't run to roses? "

Rachel did not answer, but after a moment put her hand on the gate and pushed it open. She was not looking at him, but could feel his gaze, watchful and all too perceptive, still on her face.

He swung the gate wide open for her.

" So now I'm back to Burden," he said, " knowing

nothing about him and suspecting the worst. Try to forgive me, if you can. You can get even by thinking the worst of me, like Roderick."

She went through the gate slowly. She started slowly up the road. She did not look back until she had almost reached home, then she glanced back once and saw that Neil Dalziel was still at the gate, leaning on it and watching her with a concentration that she found disturbing. The tension in her made her go rapidly the last few steps to the house.

" Rachel! " her father called from the sitting-room and came darting out. " Rachel—please, if you have to go out for some reason, don't simply vanish! Leave a note on the table, let me know where you've gone ... Yes, yes, I know that's being absurd, I know you can take care of yourself, I know there wasn't the slightest reason to worry, but at a time like this one can't help worrying. One feels anything could happen. Worry's in the air one breathes. So another time ... Please! "

He grasped her arm tightly. Rachel disengaged herself and took off her coat.

" I only went next door to take Jane the slippers she left behind, then I stayed longer than I meant to—I'm sorry," she said. " I'll get some lunch now."

" Just a minute," said Paul. " Lunch can wait. Come in here and sit down. I want to tell you about an idea I've had, an idea about that milk-bottle that was worrying you so badly."

" Oh, that milk-bottle," said Rachel, as she followed him into the living-room and sat down on the arm of a chair, showing from the way that she perched there that she meant to stay only a moment. " I don't believe it means anything." And before he could tell her his ideas about the milk-bottle, she told him her idea about Margot's fire, that there had been no firelight in Margot's room on the Saturday morning and no smoke from the chimney all the afternoon. " And that means—I'm sure it means—the fire was lit much later in the day, when it was too dark for us to see the smoke, and the curtains were drawn, so that no one would see any light in the windows."

Paul, straddling the hearthrug, fidgeting and wanting to tell her his own ideas, listened intently all the same, and when she stopped, nodded eagerly and said, " Yes, yes, yes, that fits—it's just what I was going to say. Whatever happened in the cottage happened much later than we've been thinking, because there wasn't a fire—it's very acute of you to notice that—we must tell Creed—also because the milk-bottle, which we've been thinking was taken in between the times you and I went round there actually was never taken in at all. It was pinched, that's all. I believe it was pinched by the Applin children. Bernice as good as told me so a little while ago. She practically told me the two younger ones had taken something of Miss Dalziel's, for which she'd threatened to pin their ears back and told them she wouldn't keep them out of trouble next time. And the implication of that was that she'd done her best to keep them out of trouble this time, and what I think she'd done was put the empty bottle on Brian's doorstep. That child hasn't much intelligence, but what she has is subtle and devious, and I think if she found the younger two were going to throw the bottle away in the orchard, she'd have been afraid it would be found there and would point straight at them, while a bottle on a doorstep among other bottles, would be perfectly concealed."

He stopped, smiled eagerly, delighted with his theory, then he began to feel anxious, for there was no delight on Rachel's face. There was only uncertainty and the lines of strain that sometimes showed far too plainly for her age.

" Don't you see?" he said. " There never was any possibility that Brian had helped himself to that milk— I'm sure no one could think that. And this is a really logical explanation of how the empty bottle got on to his doorstep."

" Yes, I see," she said. " No one could suspect him of helping himself to milk. Not to *milk*! " She stood up. " What are you going to do about your idea? "

" Tell Creed, naturally," Paul answered. " Or rather, I think you might tell him for me. You could telephone and tell him at the same time about the fire. But let's have lunch first. Then, while you're telephoning, I think—I think I'll go along to see the Applins. I might find it easier than the police to get Bernice to tell me the whole of the story. And I might call in on Brian on the way, to see what he thinks about it."

He had thought that that would please her. He had not seen how his coming out on Brian's side could do anything but please her. But Rachel only gave him an uneasy glance, which made him think suddenly that she was near tears, and went out. Wondering what had happened to her while she was at the cottage to bring on this difficult mood, Paul helped himself to a glass of sherry to soothe his own nerves, calling out to ask Rachel if she would like a drink too. But he received no answer. Lunch was a silent meal and Paul left immediately after it, reminding Rachel to telephone Creed.

Paul had never been into the Applin shack, but had only seen its depressing exterior and the torn lace curtains, dingy with dirt and age, that masked the teeming life inside. Nearly all the paint on the door and the window frames had flaked away, leaving only a sort of scurf on the rotting woodwork. Strange things always lay about in the garden, some old tyres, a broken hen-coop, one or two worn-out brooms, an old felt hat. It seemed that it was too much trouble to burn or bury what was no longer of any use, so it was merely thrown into the garden and left there.

As he walked down the lane towards the shack, Paul began to think about what he would say to Bernice, and to her parents, or to Mrs. Applin alone, if her husband were out. So far he had never done more than make a remark or two on the weather when he happened to meet them in the road. Applin, a small weasel of a man, with a startlingly narrow head and restless, empty eyes had always answered effusively and gone on, if Paul gave him the chance, to complain about his work, his employers, whoever they were at the moment, the cost of living and his family. Mrs. Applin, big, heavy and slow-moving and the source of her children's good looks, had never done more than mutter a surly answer. All the same, Paul thought, he would sooner have her to deal with now than the man. Somehow she kept the children well fed and healthy. She must have some good qualities. And if he could speak to her now, could sort out this business of the bottle of milk, showing her that he was not unsympathetic to the children, might he not somehow be able to establish some sort of understanding with the family, which would lead . . . ?

He stood still. Something had caught his eye in the mud of the lane, and while his thoughts still went on, full of a momentary optimism about what he might be able to do for that poor doomed child Bernice, if he really persevered, his gaze dwelt on what he had noticed at his feet. It was a threepenny bit.

He stooped to pick it up and as he did so he noticed a penny lying about two feet away. Then he saw another lying on a stone in the ditch at the side of the road. Paul picked them both up, then went on looking round for the third penny, without quite knowing why he felt that there ought to be a third. He did not find it at once, but it was because he went on looking that he saw the limp little hand in the clump of bushes.

She was there, barely hidden. There was something round her throat. Her distorted face and her clothes were caked with the mud of the lane. The sixth penny of the change that Paul had given her after buying her father's cigarettes for her lay close to the hand that protruded from the sleeve of her ragged red coat.

CHAPTER XI

PAUL STOOD quite still while the world around him gently and horribly tilted towards the abyss.

When it righted itself, it was a changed place. Neither the wind nor the creaking branches overhead seemed real. The hurrying clouds were a fantasy. A feeling of grief, profound although it was almost impersonal, took him so much by surprise that he did not seem real to himself.

After a moment he looked all round him. He had the feeling of eyes everywhere, watching. But in fact the lane was empty. Only the smoke, driven low by the wind from the chimneys of Margot Dalziel's cottage behind him and of the old barn ahead, spoke of human life near at hand. His mind began to clear and he went on to the barn.

As he reached the door he heard the ticking of a typewriter inside. It did not stop when he knocked. He knocked again. Then he could not stop himself knocking, pounding louder and louder until he heard Brian's steps inside.

The door opened and Brian looked out with a scowl at the interruption.

" Yes, what is it? " he asked with irritable anxiety.

" Come with me, will you? " Paul said, turned at once and started back to the spot where Bernice lay among the bushes.

His mind was hardly on Brian at all, yet he realised that there was something unusual about him. His face looked drained and pale and had a heaviness and a redness of the eyes which told of lack of sleep. He followed Paul with obvious unwillingness, deliberately staying a little way behind him until he caught sight of the red coat and the muddied, crumpled thing inside it. Then he went past Paul in a few long strides, knelt among the thorns and put a hand against the contorted face.

113

" Cold," he said in a voice that was only just audible.
" When did it happen? "

" I don't know. I saw her this morning. We talked for
a little while. She was with the other two. . . ." Paul felt
unnecessary words beginning to gush out of him, the
stream released by shock. Somehow he made them stop.
" Will you go to the cottage, Brian, and telephone the
police? I'll stay here."

Brian stood up, took a step backwards, but as if he
could not take his eyes off the dead child, went on staring
blankly at her.

Paul put a sharper authority into his voice. " We've got
to get the police immediately, and one of us must stay
here. You can get along faster than I can. Will you go to
the cottage and telephone? "

" I'll go straight to Gower himself," said Brian, yet
still he stood there, his face bemused and incredulous.

" The telephone would be quicker," said Paul.

Brian muttered something in reply which Paul did not
catch. When Paul asked him what he had said, Brian's
features twitched as if he had momentarily forgotten
that Paul was there and found his presence an annoy-
ance.

" Nothing, nothing," he said in the same almost
inaudible voice. " ' The doubly dead ', I said. ' A
dirge for her, the doubly dead, in that she died so
young. . . .' That's all. Nothing. Kevin can't have done
this, can he? "

" *Kevin?* " said Paul. That the brother could have
murdered his sister had not even crossed his mind.

" What happened then? " asked Brian.

" Look, are you going? " said Paul. He realised that it
would probably be quicker to go himself, but he had an
extreme unwillingness to leave Brian alone here. " The
first thing is to get the police."

Without another word Brian turned and set off down
the lane.

Paul saw that he was not making for the cottage, which

114

he could have reached by pushing through a gap in the hedge into the orchard, but was going to the village.

" Use the telephone, damn you! " Paul shouted after him.

Brian only lengthened his strides and went on.

Paul found himself shaking in helpless anger because Brian had not done what he had told him. Then it occurred to him that possibly Brian had been right in not going to the cottage, for if he had done so it would have brought Roderick and Jane rushing out together, and Paul would not have welcomed that at all at the moment. But although his anger subsided, the shaking did not stop and his inability to control it began to make him angry with himself. Walking a little way off, he leant against a tree trunk and tried to force himself to think lucidly about what had happened.

He found that the only thing that he could think of was Brian's determination not to go to the cottage. Brian had been so much in his thoughts for the last few days that having him there was becoming a habit, an approach to an obsession. Yet Paul had not thought about him coherently and usefully. He had not pondered the strange fact that from the time of Margot Dalziel's disappearance, Brian had neither gone to the cottage nor tried to see the Hardwickes. He had stayed in his barn. He had kept out of everyone's way, working perhaps, or perhaps merely trying to stay out of sight, to avoid trouble. In any case, it was egotistical, cold-hearted behaviour, even worse than Paul would have expected from him. And it might be very unwise behaviour too, for sooner or later it was bound to draw attention to him.

The gusts of wind cut into Paul like spears as he stood waiting, and presently he began to hear Bernice's voice wailing with them, her shrill voice, shrieking at her sisters, as she ran away from him and vanished into the lane. There must have been another scream after those shouts, he thought, which had been drowned by this infernal wind.

He wondered about the other two children. Had they run straight home, or had they seen anything or heard anything? Even if they had, even if they had actually seen their sister killed in the lane, it was unlikely that they would have anything useful to say about it. Terror and bewilderment would have emptied their poor little minds of what little was normally in them.

All of a sudden Paul remembered what had brought him out this afternoon, why he was in the lane at all. He had been going to see the Applins. He had been going to find out if he could induce Bernice to tell him anything about the missing milk-bottle. Well, there was nothing to be done about that now. Yet someone would have to go to see the Applins. But fortunately that was a job for the police. Paul's only duty at the moment was to stay where he was, which, heaven knew, was hard enough. The sound of Gower's motor bicycle in the lane was one of the most welcome that he had ever heard.

Gower was by himself, but Brian returned soon after him, and while Paul told Gower how he had found the body, went silently past him and Paul to his door. There Brian paused, then turned, came a little way back and stood watching and listening.

Gower just then was considering the muddy coins that Paul had given him, with an account of how Bernice had happened to have the money with her.

" So it happened soon after she left you, Mr. Hard-wicke," said Gower. " She never got home. If she'd got home she'd have handed the money over to the old woman."

" That's how it looks," said Paul.

" So she met someone in the lane. If he'd been following her, you'd have seen him, wouldn't you? "

" I think so, unless, of course, she came back to the main road after I'd gone home."

" But you said she was running, shouting after the others. Why'd she come back? "

" I'm not saying she did," said Paul. " It just occurred

to me she might have. Her starting to shout and running away was a bit of an act to get away from me when she realised I was beginning to lecture her for her own good. But once she'd got away, I don't know what mightn't have come into her head."

" That's right," said Gower. " That's something you'd never be able to guess."

" For instance," said Paul, " there was a car in the lane, I remember. I think it was Mr. Dalziel's car— Miss Dalziel's brother's, I mean, not her nephew's. But I'm no good at identifying cars, so I can't swear to it. There was a car there, anyway, parked a few yards down the lane, and Bernice might have come back to take a look at it."

" Why would Mr. Dalziel have parked his car there instead of in Miss Dalziel's drive? " asked Gower.

" I don't know," said Paul. " As I said, it may not have been his at all."

Gower turned towards Brian. " Did you see or hear anything unusual around that time, Mr. Burden? "

" No," said Brian, coming a few steps nearer, " but I was working and it's surprising how little else you hear when you've a typewriter going."

" You never saw Bernice herself this afternoon, or the two younger ones either? " Gower asked. " They never came to your door or anything like that? "

" No," said Brian. " Not this afternoon. Why should they? "

" Didn't you have them around a good deal? "

" Oh yes, all the time."

" But not this afternoon? "

" Not any time to-day. I saw Kevin——" Brian stopped.

" When did you see Kevin? " Gower asked.

" Sometime in the morning," said Brian. " Sometime after you people had been along, questioning him about what he'd been doing on Saturday."

" Any special reason why he came? "

" I don't think so, except to blow off steam about being persecuted by the police, and not being given a chance to go straight, and so on."

" Ah," said Gower. " Did he happen to mention that he was clearing out? "

" No," said Brian. " Has he cleared out? "

" Looks a bit like it," said Gower.

Brian came another few steps closer. " Look, Gower, Kevin can't have had anything to do with *that*." He made a jerky gesture at the patch of brambles. " The Applins hang together. He might have blacked the girl's eye in one of his ugly moods, but he'd never—never have . . ."

The words died away with a strange uncertainty.

It was then that Fred Harper, one of the constables in the village, arrived and a few minutes afterwards the first police car came down the lane with Creed in it.

Paul, waiting to be questioned again or told to go home, withdrew a little way up the lane. He saw Fred Harper sent off to tell the Applins what had happened. He saw the doctor come and crouch down among the brambles. Presently Neil Dalziel appeared and came to Paul's side. He did not speak at first, but stood intently watching the movements of the men around the child's dead body.

Finally he asked, " Who is she? "

" Bernice Applin," said Paul. " A girl from a cottage down the lane."

There was another pause, then Dalziel asked, " Rape? "

Paul was remembering that he had just been telling Gower that it might have been this man's car that had been in the lane when Bernice went running down it. " I don't know," he said. " What brought you here just now? "

" I'd just stopped at the cottage when I saw the police car with the inspector in it come tearing down here," said Dalziel. " I jumped to the conclusion that it was something to do with my sister."

" Perhaps it is," said Paul.

Dalziel turned his head to look at him. " How could it be? "

" If the child saw something. . . ."

Dalziel's long stare continued.

" She was always around the cottage, you see," said Paul. " She may have been the one person who really knew what happened there."

Dalziel shook his head, dismissing the suggestion, which intensely irritated Paul and made him suddenly quite certain that he had hit on the right explanation of the murder. He began to tell Dalziel his conclusions about the milk-bottle.

Dalziel interrupted. " Why should she have kept whatever she saw to herself? "

" She may not have understood it."

" She'd have understood it all right if she'd seen Margot being knocked about."

" She may not have seen that. She may merely have seen someone here who's supposed to have been somewhere else, or something of that sort. As I was saying, if the children took the bottle——"

But again Paul was interrupted, this time by Roderick, who came from the orchard, pushing his way through the hedge, with Jane behind him.

They both stood staring at the group of policemen, then Jane turned and ran away with both hands pressed to her mouth. Roderick gave an uneasy look after her, then came a few steps forward.

" Who is it? " he asked, the words coming huskily out of a dry throat.

" Bernice Applin," said Paul.

" Oh—one of them," said Roderick.

" But I'd go after your wife, if I were you," said Paul. " You can't do anything here."

Roderick stayed where he was. " Why was she . . . ? "

" I think she saw something," said Paul. " She was

hanging around the cottage on Saturday morning. She may have seen who came here with Miss Dalziel."

Brian had joined them. " Or who didn't," he said. " Roderick, if you aren't going to look after Jane, I will."

" Oh—thanks," said Roderick, still vague, still only half on the spot, and as Brian thrust through the gap in the hedge, he asked, " What did he mean—who didn't? Who didn't what?"

" Who didn't come here with Miss Dalziel," said Paul. " I think he believes she came here alone, set up that scene we found and then cleared out. Or he's pretending he believes that."

" No," Roderick muttered incredulously. " He can't believe that."

" Well, he's almost convinced Rachel of it," said Paul.

" No!" Roderick's voice rose and began to shake. "Jane said that too—something like that. You're all saying Margot went mad. Because of me. Then came back and murdered that girl, because she saw it all. Don't you realise that's what you're saying?"

" I'm not," said Dalziel dryly. " I don't believe the two things have anything to do with each other. This is going to turn out a fairly commonplace crime."

" Commonplace—my God!" said Roderick, with a convulsive shudder.

" In the sense that it seems to have happened almost every time one reads a newspaper," said Dalziel.

" You're a cold-blooded swine," said Roderick.

" Perhaps," said Dalziel. " Yes, I dare say."

" Margot said so too," said Roderick.

" Probably having just made my blood run cold herself," said Dalziel. " Now who are these? The Applin parents? We'd better go, hadn't we? This is a family occasion."

He walked away and Roderick uncertainly followed him.

But Paul stood watching the two Applins coming along

the lane. The man was ahead, hurrying and stumbling. Shrill, unintelligible words dribbled out of his mouth. His face was yellow with shock and his eyes stared blankly. His wife strode heavily after him with Fred Harper beside her. She had no coat on, but only a cotton overall hanging unbuttoned over a soiled woollen dress. Her feet plodded through the mud of the lane in blue felt slippers, trimmed with pink fur. Her grey hair was bundled up in a hair-net.

Until she was a few feet from her daughter's body her face showed almost nothing, although her eyes were fixed on the spot where Bernice lay, then all of a sudden all the strength went out of her sullen features, she gave a loud cry and plunged forward.

Gower stopped her, his arms going round her.

" Now then, Nell," he said quietly. " Now then, my dear."

She became as still as stone, staring past him at Bernice.

" You shouldn't have come," he said. " You should have stopped at home with the kids."

" Think I could stop her? " cried Applin querulously, looking everywhere with his wild staring eyes except at his daughter. " I told her, I said, ' You stop home, Nell.' I said, ' You stop home, I'll see to this.' Didn't I, Fred? " he appealed to Harper. " Didn't I? "

" You! " she said in a voice hoarse with contempt.

It was the only thing she said all the time that she stood there, while Gower was trying to persuade her to go home again, with something in his voice that intrigued Paul, a gentleness, an intimacy that went beyond mere sympathy for her in her grief. He thought of Gower's neat, pretty wife, his two bright, well-dressed children, his comfortable home, and then found himself wondering when the sergeant had known Nell Applin well enough to be able to speak to her like that.

She gave no sign of responding to it, but at last she

looked up. Tears were running out of her eyes as she turned her head, looking at the other policemen, one after the other, then past them to where Paul stood, a little way up the lane.

Her husband was still chattering. " I don't know what we'll do now. First our Kevin gone off and now this. Kevin gone off, we don't know where, and now Bernice. Kevin wouldn't stay. He wouldn't stay, he said, not with the police at him again when he done nothing. He said ' I'm off,' he said, ' I'm not staying around with them always at me.' And now . . ."

The flow stopped as Applin realised that his wife's stare had remained fixed on Paul. For a moment Applin was silent, thought working painfully inside his oddly shaped, narrow head, then he raised a fist and started shaking it at Paul.

" That's right! " he shouted. " That's right! That's him! The kids told us. They told us, ' Mr. Hardwicke's got hold of Bernice,' they said. ' He give her money and she's gone off with Mr. Hardwicke! ' "

CHAPTER XII

BEFORE HE had time to think, Paul experienced panic. It froze his joints and cut off his breath and turned the faces of the men who were looking at him into grotesque masks of enmity.

Luckily the feeling came and went all in a moment and the face of Walter Creed, as he came towards Paul, regained its normal look of cautious detachment. No frightful suspicion blazed in his eyes. They were merely as non-committal as usual, the doubt in them directed at himself as much as at Paul.

" Gower's been telling me what you told him," said

Creed. " The children saw you talking to Bernice after she came into the pub, didn't they? "

" Yes, we chatted for a moment while the two younger children ran off home," said Paul. " But Bernice followed them almost immediately."

" Gower says you mentioned a car in the lane."

" Yes, a black car," said Paul.

" I'd like to hear more about that," said Creed, " but if you want to go home, I'll call round presently."

Paul took that as a way of telling him that at the moment he was a little under Creed's feet. Saying that whenever Creed came, he would find him at home, he set off along the lane, stamping his feet to warm them as he went, but feeling so chilled that it seemed possible that nothing would ever thaw his blood again.

He found Rachel in the sitting-room, curled up, half-asleep, in a chair by the fire. He saw that she had started to write some letters, for there were some sheets of paper and a packet of envelopes on a small table beside her, but she must have given up the effort almost at once, for except for half a page, that was nearly all crossing out, she had written nothing.

She roused herself drowsily as Paul came in and said that she had tried to telephone Creed but had been told that he was not available. " Have you been to the Applins? " she asked.

" No," said Paul and suddenly feeling that it would be impossible for him to say a word about what had happened he sat down, put his face in his hands, and let out a loud groan.

He heard it in the quiet room, a horrible sound, all self-pitying weakness, like his moment of blind terror in the lane. Dropping his hands and trying to make out that he had been smothering a yawn, he said, " No, Rachel, I had my idea too late. Things had happened already. That child Bernice . . ."

He saw horror growing on Rachel's face as he paused

again and realised that his own face was probably telling her most of what he had to say.

"In a patch of brambles," he went on. "Dead. Strangled, I think. The police are there. Creed's coming round presently."

Rachel's eyes opened wider, but she said nothing, for which Paul was grateful. He dropped his head into his hands again.

After a short silence she stood up and said in a far-away voice, "I'll make some tea."

The door opened and closed.

Paul sat still for a minute, then stood up and began to pace up and down the room. He kept seeing again the movement of the heads of all the men in the lane when that fantastic accusation had been shouted at him, but now, in his mind's eye, the faces were all blank. They had neither expression nor individuality. They had turned into identical blobs of featureless clay, to which it would be hopeless to explain oneself, with which it would be useless to reason.

"This is awful," Paul said aloud. "This is ridiculous. No one could believe . . . Of course not. No one could possibly imagine . . ."

But those blank threatening faces merely turned slightly, so that they could follow him about the room, like the sea of faces following the ball at a tennis match.

To have something else to think about, Paul picked up the scribbled sheet of paper that Rachel had left on the table by her chair, and read, "Dear Dr. Fergusson, Would it be possible for me to see you any day next week? I have been considering the possibility . . ."

There was no need to read any further. Paul realised that Rachel had been trying to draft a letter, asking for her old job back. He put the sheet of paper down and was again walking up and down the room, trying to find courage to defy those blank faces as well as the new fear that the letter had suddenly brought to him, when Rachel returned with the tea.

She seemed to have been shocked out of curiosity and only murmured as she sat down, " This wind—I hate it! I prefer the frost. At least it's quiet."

She did not mention that every time the wind whistled in the chimney, she heard Bernice shrieking in the lane and remembered herself thinking of a banshee and of death, yet doing nothing about it. It would, perhaps, have been rather difficult to know just what to do about a banshee, yet a person of more imagination, she felt, might have responded to something in the air. She had merely gone on unconcernedly to the cottage with Jane's slippers and had sat calmly listening to her chattering nonsense about Margot Dalziel getting drunk by herself and smashing the place up and disappearing with an imaginary lover, while horrors were being perpetrated within a stone's throw.

Remaining in the silence of their separate nightmares, both Rachel and Paul were relieved when the bell rang and Mrs. Godfrey came in.

She had heard of the murder, she said, in the village shop, where she always picked up a great deal of information.

" If ever I treat myself to a refrigerator, I don't know what I'll do," she said, sitting down and gratefully accepting a cup of tea. " I'd only have to shop once or twice a week, instead of practically every day, and I'd never keep up with what was going on. They were all talking in there just now as if they'd expected this horrible business. They were saying something of the sort was certain to happen to the poor child sooner or later, neglected as she was. They're assuming it's a sex crime, of course."

" That's by no means certain—not at all! " cried Paul. His voice was angrily defensive and his face had begun to burn. He wondered what else Mrs. Godfrey had been told in the shop. What else was already being said in the village?

But her sensible, crisp voice, as she went on, was soothing.

" They're such a tragedy, that family. I remember Nell Applin when she was a girl—Nell Burt she was then. One of the loveliest girls you ever saw, in that black-haired, red cheeked, gypsyish way. She was never very bright, but she was a good-humoured, well brought up girl, who came to church every Sunday in a pretty straw hat with flowers on it and a clean pair of gloves. She could have had any young man in the village, including Jim Gower, even after that little rat Applin got her in the family way. But the Burts were terribly respectable people and they got her married to Applin in a hurry, imagining they would go away and live in Fallford, where he was supposed to have a job of sorts. They did go away, but they were back within the year, living in that dump they've been in ever since, with Applin in and out of work every few months, and producing more and more Applins. And poor Nell became what she is now." Mrs. Godfrey drank some tea. " If it wasn't a sex crime, Mr. Hardwicke, what was it? "

" Perhaps something to do with this mystery of what's happened to Miss Dalziel," said Paul. " Bernice was always around the cottage."

" Ah yes," said Mrs. Godfrey, " that place must have been a terrible temptation to the children, empty half the time. And when Miss Dalziel first came to live here, I remember she rather encouraged them. She was sorry for them, naturally, and used to think up little jobs to give them, for which she then paid them far too much. So of course they were in and out all the time. It wasn't until Bernice started selling her flowers that came from the churchyard that Miss Dalziel decided things had gone too far."

Rachel gave a start. " From the *churchyard*? "

" Yes, indeed," said Mrs. Godfrey. " I happened to call on Miss Dalziel just after she'd bought a nice bunch of border carnations from the children, and I thought I recognised them as some from my own garden, which I'd given to my Mrs. Waters—she comes in on Tuesdays and Saturdays and she's so good and reliable, I don't know what I'd do without her—well, I'd given them to her to put on her mother's grave. She always has a bunch of flowers from my garden on a Saturday morning to take to the churchyard, because Mr. Waters won't grow anything in their own garden he can't eat, and Mrs. Waters generally brings me a lettuce, or some beans or some such thing in exchange. Well, when she and I looked into the matter of these carnations, sure enough, the ones I'd given her weren't on her mother's grave any more, so we considered that sufficient proof and I thought I'd better tell Miss Dalziel where her flowers had come from. After that I think she felt she'd had enough of the Applins."

Rachel pointed at the dahlias.

" I bought those from Bernice on Sunday morning," she said. " I guessed she'd pinched them somewhere, but I never thought of the churchyard."

" Well, it wasn't necessarily the churchyard," said Mrs. Godfrey. " It might have been any of our gardens—Miss Dalziel's, perhaps. I noticed last week she had a nice bed of dahlias."

" But not on Sunday," said Rachel. " They'd all been killed by the frost on Friday night."

" That's true," said Paul. " I remember noticing them when I dropped in at the cottage on Saturday morning and thinking they ought to have been lifted. They were a dreadful mess."

" Yes, of course—I was forgetting the frost," said Mrs. Godfrey. " All our dahlias around here were killed, if they hadn't been lifted already, so I suppose these came from a shop and I don't know where Bernice would have got hold of flowers from a shop unless it was in the churchyard."

Rachel stood up. " I think perhaps I'll go and put them in the dust-bin," she said. " They're beginning to have a depressing effect on me."

" No," said Paul, " leave them where they are. We'll have to tell Creed about them."

" But it was on Sunday I bought them," said Rachel. " He won't be interested in what Bernice was doing on Sunday, will he? I thought Saturday was the important day."

" We don't know," said Paul. " Anything Bernice did during the last few days of her life may turn out to be important."

Important or not, Creed, who appeared about an hour later, listened with interest to what Paul and Rachel had to tell him about the dahlias, while the young detective who had arrived with him, took notes.

Paul also told Creed of his belief that it was the Applin children who had taken the milk-bottle from Miss Dalziel's doorstep, and of Rachel's that no fire had been lit in the cottage on Saturday, at least until after dark.

Mrs. Godfrey had left before Creed arrived and dusk was falling. The wind still buffeted the windows and found chinks under the doors, and Rachel, sitting by the fire, felt draughts biting coldly at her ankles. While Creed and her father talked, she began to think about buying some copper strip to fix to the doorways. But then she thought suddenly of Margot Dalziel's barn, which needed so much more than copper strip to make it draught-proof, and that led her to thinking of Brian and so of the letter that she had started to write to Dr. Fergusson, asking if there was any chance that she could have her old job back. The unfinished draft lay on the table by her chair. Picking it up, she crumpled it and threw it into the fire.

Creed was saying to her father, " I understand it's practically certain the girl wasn't sexually assaulted. She was killed quickly and neatly with a length of electric flex. And that brings us back to the question of Miss Dalziel's disappearance and whether or not Bernice knew anything about it. So you're quite right that everything to do with her movements on Saturday and Sunday becomes important. Now let me go over what you've just told me and see if I've got it straight."

He glanced at the other detective, who turned a page in his notebook and nodded.

"You yourself, Mr. Hardwicke," said Creed, "saw Bernice and her sisters in the garden of the cottage on Saturday morning, just before the milk was delivered. You turned them out, but you don't know whether or not they came back again."

"No," said Paul.

"And this morning Bernice hinted to you that her sisters had taken something of Miss Dalziel's and you believe it was the milk-bottle."

"Yes."

"Which removes the only piece of evidence we have which suggests that Miss Dalziel came down on Saturday morning."

"Exactly."

"Nevertheless, if she was there, or if anyone else was there then, Bernice may have seen them."

"Yes."

"On the other hand, Miss Hardwicke now remembers there was no smoke coming from the cottage chimney on Saturday morning when she took over a bottle of milk at about half past twelve."

"And no firelight in the sitting-room and no smoke all the afternoon," said Paul. "She was in the garden until it began to grow dark and she's certain she'd have noticed it if she'd seen smoke suddenly streaming out."

"So you believe the fire was lit, whether by Miss Dalziel or somebody else, later in the evening."

"Or it could have been earlier in the morning," said Paul. "Quite early, before we were up. Only there's the sherry. I'm sure Miss Dalziel wouldn't have thought of drinking sherry at that hour."

"The evening certainly seems to have been the likeliest time for her to have arrived," said Creed. "And so we get around to the question of whether or not Bernice Applin saw anything on Saturday evening, or even on Sunday morning."

" You could try asking her sisters," said Paul. " They were probably with her, wherever she was."

" I'd be surprised if we got anything intelligible out of them," said Creed. " But if at least we could find out where she got those dahlias . . ."

He stopped. He gave his tight-lipped smile.

" I was just thinking," he went on. " I like flowers all right, but just sometimes one can have too many of them. We're also trying to find out where those yellow roses were bought, you know. They're dealing with that for us in London."

" Because, if you can find out who bought them, you've got your murderer? "

" I don't know about that. Miss Dalziel may have bought them herself. But if she did, finding out where may tell us something about her movements."

" I suppose it isn't possible there's some connection between the roses and the dahlias," said Paul. " I mean that they came from the same shop."

Creed looked again at the dahlias. " I don't know, but that doesn't look to me the sort of bunch you'd buy from a florist. They're different lengths and the kinds are all mixed up, cactus and decorative, and shops generally seem to sell you all of one sort. Still, it's an idea. I'll bear it in mind."

" But the frost killed off most of the flowers in the gardens round here, so they must have come from a shop of some sort," said Paul, " even if it wasn't as smart a place as the one that sold the roses. Perhaps it was one in Fallford, the kind that's a grocer and a green-grocer and a bit of everything else, and gets its supplies from some local nursery. If they'd got the dahlias in on Friday, before the frost, and sold them on Saturday to someone from the village here, who took them along to the church-yard on Sunday on the way to church——"

"Wait a minute, wait a minute!" Creed slid forward to the edge of his chair. "You've just given me an idea, Mr. Hardwicke. A local nursery. Kevin Applin went to see Browder, his old employer, on Saturday morning. Browder's a market-gardener. If it was Kevin . . ."

But at that point a change came over Creed's face. Deliberately, it seemed to Paul as he watched him, Creed quenched the spark of excitement.

"Just an idea," said Creed, his greenish eyes becoming so non-committal as to look quite stupid. "I must think about it. And now, Miss Hardwicke, would you mind telling me a little more about your visit to Miss Dalziel's cottage this afternoon?"

Rachel had to make an effort to bring her thoughts back to him and to what he was asking her. Since she had tossed the draft of her letter into the fire, she had been fumblingly trying to understand the impulse that had made her write. She would have said at the time that she had suddenly decided to make a clean break with Brian. Yet really that had had very little to do with it. For Brian himself would soon be leaving the barn, would be going to London.

"My visit this afternoon . . . ?" she said.

"When you realised about the smoke and the fire," said Creed.

"What else do you want to know about it?" she asked.

"Mainly who was there."

"Mrs. Dalziel was there," said Rachel, "and Miss Dalziel's brother—only, as a matter of fact, I'm not quite sure when he arrived. Mrs. Dalziel didn't seem to know about it. We just found him in the sitting-room, looking at the books, when we went in. He seems to think some of them have been stolen. And Roderick Dalziel came in a little while later. He'd been to the village to buy some food."

"What about Mr. Burden? Did you see him?"

"No."

Creed turned to Paul. "Did you see any of these people

as you went home after talking to the girl? " he asked.
" Or anyone else? "

" No," said Paul. " I only saw the car I told Gower
about parked just inside the lane."

Creed stood up. " That's all then, I think, for the
moment, but I'd like to take those dahlias with me."

As Rachel took them out of the vase, he looked at Paul
again.

" You'll be here, will you, if we should want to get in
touch with you again? " he asked.

" Yes, yes, of course." Paul, hurrying ahead to the
door, was wishing that Creed had said something about
the Applins' fantastic accusation, had said at least a word
or two about it, so that Paul could have brushed it aside.
He could not manage to speak of it himself, could not
bring out a single question. He knew that if he tried
to do so, his voice would start to shake and give away the
unreasonable terror with which Applin's screaming voice
had filled him.

Opening the front door for Creed with a jerk that
betrayed the tension of his nerves, he said, " And if there's
anything further we can do at any time . . ." He stopped
in mid-sentence.

A woman whom he had never seen before, an unusually
tall and heavily built woman, was at the gate. The light
that fell upon her from the doorway showed up a square,
harsh-featured face and wispy grey hair. She was wearing
muddy gumboots, a tweed suit with a short, sagging skirt
and a square-shouldered, double-breasted jacket. She
came striding up to the door and although Paul did not
know her, he saw at once that Creed unquestionably did,
for his face showed more emotion than Paul had ever
seen on it before, and all of a sudden he was in a great
hurry to be gone.

Seeming to make his spare form even narrower than it
was, he managed to dodge between the woman and the
doorpost, saying as he disappeared into the darkness,
" Ah, good evening, Mrs. Meredith. You're looking for

your daughter, I expect. I hope not for me. An important appointment . . ."

With a puzzled frown on her high, square forehead, the woman turned to look after him and the young detective, who was carrying the dahlias and keeping close at Creed's heels. Paul saw with astonishment that her bewilderment brought out an astonishing resemblance to Jane. It was as if someone very like that quivering bird of a girl was trapped inside this woman's self-confidence and solid muscle.

" Mr. Hardwicke? " she said. Her voice was more of a pipe than Paul had been expecting, but it was the sort of high voice which, without being raised, always drowns all others. No one else would ever be able to talk when Mrs. Meredith wished to do so. " Creed might at least have stayed to introduce us. I'd heard he was on the job. Very unfortunate. We shan't get anywhere. He's got no imagination and no real thoroughness to make up for it. Whenever I see him he's in a hurry, dashing off to the next thing without any particularly good reason. I think I'll speak to Sir Arthur about it—Sir Arthur Frisby, our Chief Constable, you know. A really first class man. A very strong character, yet so humane." She became aware that Paul was trying to say something to her. " Oh no, thank you, I won't come in," she said. " My boots." She pointed down at them.

Paul said that they were of no consequence.

" Are you sure? " she said. " They're pretty muddy. I tell you what, I'll take them off. Have to apologise for my stockings, but it's better than leaving mud all over your carpets. I'd just got back from taking the dogs for a run when some men from Fallford turned up to ask me a lot of questions about when Jane and Roderick arrived on Saturday. That was the first my husband and I heard about all this trouble. Jane, of course, wouldn't dream of letting us know anything and we haven't got television. Can't afford it. And I can't always be bothered with the papers. Nothing but the bomb nowadays and all this sitting down and marching about. High-principled, of course. I respect them for it. Still, I've got tired of it all. Nothing new ever seems to happen."

She was struggling out of her boots. When she was free of them, she left them standing like a pair of sentries on the doormat and tramped inside. She had very long, thin feet and the nail of one big toe showed through a hole in the heavily ribbed stockings that she was wearing.

Meeting Rachel in the doorway of the living-room and shaking hands with her, she said, " Awfully sorry about my stockings and there wasn't really any need for me to come in at all. I only came to thank you for being so helpful to Jane and Roderick yesterday. I've just been to the cottage to tell them to get packed up and come home with me, and Jane told me how kind you'd been. Immensely kind. I can't tell you how grateful I am, though I'd have been even more grateful if someone had thought of getting in touch with me. The idea of those two children trying to cope with all this mess by themselves! "

Her voice was beginning to get on Paul's nerves. It seemed to be sawing through his ear-drums. He was at one with King Lear, he decided, on the subject of women's voices.

" Everyone has to start coping alone, sooner or later," he said.

" Ah, you're dead right, of course," she said. " All the young need plenty of independence. I always saw to it that Jane had all she could manage from the day she was born. Never any ordering about without a complete explanation of why I wanted her to do what I did, never even any cleanliness training. But she hasn't a grain of sense all the same, except that I must say my husband and I were pleasantly surprised by Roderick. When the child first started to tell us she'd got married, we were both horribly afraid she was going to say it was to that impossible young man she introduced to Miss Dalziel and persuaded her to let live in that old barn of hers. You probably know him, a big, grubby sort of young man who pretends to write books. The child seemed to be absolutely infatuated with him, and we've often trembled to think how far things might have gone between them, apart from his getting most of Jane's salary out of her. We've even wondered if all this independence was really a good thing after all. But then, to our vast relief, she turned up with Roderick."

She drew breath for a moment. Paul did not dare to look at Rachel, but sensing the sudden stiffening of her body, he started to say hurriedly that he supposed Mrs. Meredith had heard about the tragedy in the lane that afternoon.

Her strident voice drowned his. "Quiet and nice mannered, I thought, even if he's rather younger and more obviously inexperienced than I'd have chosen for Jane. But still, there was his aunt in the background, I thought, to whom Jane's always been devoted and who's always had an excellent influence on her. A really intelligent sort of woman, I'm sure you agree with me. A terrible thing if anything's happened to her. But if it has . . ."

She gave a grim smile, and advancing to the fire, held one of her stockinged feet close to it and wiggled the long, flexible toes.

"If it has, at least they won't have far to look for the culprit," she said. "Creed may be too blinded by Burden's quite good accent to think it's possible and he's probably trying to incriminate some unfortunate village lad. But as it happens, I know a thing or two about Burden and fortunately I've got the ear of Sir Arthur."

CHAPTER XIII

CREED WAS in one of his moods on the drive back to Fallford. The young man who was with him recognised the signs of it and kept his thoughts to himself.

Frowning in what looked like deep concentration, Creed was in fact indulging a fantasy. In it he had irrefutable evidence that Mrs. Meredith had committed the murders of Margot Dalziel and Bernice Applin and as his investigations continued, he found not only more and more evidence against her, such as a number of valuable stolen books hidden in her home under copies of *Country Life*, and a thick walking-stick, tossed carelessly in a corner amongst mackintoshes and boots, with some of Margot Dalziel's curly grey hair sticking to it, but also more and more murdered bodies. All the people who had disappeared from the area in even faintly mysterious circumstances during all Creed's lifetime as a policeman, kept turning up dead somewhere in the Meredith's charming, ramshackle, Georgian house. From cupboards, from attics, from under the curving stairs and from behind worm-eaten panelling, Creed brought them all out. It made him feel a good deal better.

At the same time he remembered that Mrs. Meredith was an appalling trouble-maker and that he would have to watch his step. She loved tripping up the police and making them appear ridiculous. Probably a frustrated policewoman herself, he thought, grinning to himself as he hurled some of her half-digested psychology back in her face. God knew what romantic daydreams she went in for of tempting some undetected sexual maniac into some dark alley, then settling his hash with a smart piece of judo.

At the moment, for instance, if she had somehow heard

of Applin's accusation of that amiable old fool Hardwicke, she might at this moment be trying to lure him out into the night. . . .

Creed emerged abruptly from his own daydream, feeling ashamed of himself. There he went as usual, taking too much for granted. He had no real proof of Paul Hardwicke's amiability and stranger things than his turning out to be a murderer were always happening. So an open mind had to be maintained at all costs, if you didn't want a Mrs. Meredith to be able to make a fool of you. It just happened to be a pity that an open mind was a most uninspiring thing to be saddled with.

When the car reached the police-station in Fallford, Creed found Neil Dalziel waiting for him. He also found a report from London on his desk. Perhaps because of his continuing uneasiness about Mrs. Meredith's appearance on the scene, he felt a need to assert his own power, and did so by studying the report first and keeping Neil Dalziel waiting.

He saw that Roderick Dalziel's statements about his movements from Friday to Sunday had been more or less corroborated by several people. Roderick had met his aunt at London Airport on Friday afternoon and had driven her home to her flat. They had stopped on the way and gone into a flower shop together and Miss Dalziel had bought a dozen chrysanthemums. The Crosbys, the couple who lived in the basement flat below Margot Dalziel's, had heard her and Roderick arrive together, hearing first their voices in the street, then their footsteps overhead, and then, at about six o'clock, Miss Dalziel had appeared at the Crosbys' door and invited them upstairs for a drink to celebrate her nephew's marriage.

The Crosbys both said that she had been obviously tired, yet in a particularly gay and happy mood. They had stayed for about an hour, then had gone downstairs to their own supper. They thought it was about half past ten when Roderick left. They had heard him call out good night from the doorway and go to his car and drive away. Soon afterwards the Crosbys had gone to bed. They always went to bed early, because they both had to be in their offices at nine o'clock in the morning, but Mr. Crosby, waking presently and seeing on the luminous dial of the alarm clock that it was nearly midnight, had heard Miss Dalziel's bath water running and all the usual sounds of her going to bed.

So that made it fairly sure, Creed thought, that the fire in her cottage hadn't been lit early on Saturday morning. It was the evening that was important. Saturday evening.

He read on. The Crosbys had not heard Miss Dalziel leave the house, because as usual they had left it themselves long before she would have been up, but she had apparently been gone by the time that they returned for lunch, for there had been no more sounds overhead. The rest of Roderick's story, his arrival at his own lodgings in the evening, his staying there all the next morning, his lunch at the restaurant in the Euston Road, his arrival at the Merediths' house at tea-time, had been confirmed by his landlady, by a waiter at the restaurant, by Brigadier and Mrs. Meredith. It all seemed quite straightforward.

Yet there was one part of it that worried Creed. There seemed to be no doubt that Roderick had stayed in his lodgings all Saturday morning, for several people had vouched for it, but why had he done so? Jane had gone home to break the news of her marriage to her parents on Friday evening. Her movements from the time she had left the office until the time when her father had met her at Fallford station had been easy to trace. And perhaps it was understandable that she should have wanted to handle her parents alone. But on Saturday morning she had apparently had nothing much to do, had merely taken the family car and gone into Fallford to do a little shopping. So why had Roderick not followed her in the morning? Why had he waited about, gossiping to his landlady and the other lodgers, instead of driving off straight after breakfast to join his wife?

That morning, Creed remembered, was the time about which she had been a bit shifty when he questioned her. So could it have been Jane who had arranged things so that Roderick should not come down until the afternoon? Had she meant to be up to something on her own in the morning? Or had he stayed in London because he was supposed to pick up his aunt and drive her down? Was that it? Had he driven her down?

Creed's study of the map, however, had convinced him that if Roderick had not left London until after his lunch at Cirio's, he could not possibly have reached Miss Dalziel's cottage, murdered her there, loaded her body into his car and dumped it somewhere on the way back to the Merediths' house, arriving there by half past four, as it was certain that he had. The journey was a hundred and twenty-five miles, the early part of it through London traffic. That was a theory of the crime that need not even be considered.

Yet at that point, reading on, Creed's certainty was jolted. The report ended with the statement that at three-thirty on the Saturday afternoon a young man answering to the description of Roderick Dalziel, had bought a dozen yellow roses from a florist in a certain suburban shopping-centre on the main road from London to Fallford.

Creed read it with dismay. It made no sense. If that young man had been Roderick, he had driven straight from that shop to the Merediths'. There had been no time for him to do anything else. And if both Brigadier Meredith and his wife stated that their son-in-law had not left their house until the next morning, Creed was prepared to believe them. So when could Roderick have given the roses to his aunt? Was it possible that she had been waiting in the car while he went into the shop and that he had given them to her straight away, that he had then dropped her at some point on the journey and she somehow made her way home alone, or with someone else? If so, why had Roderick not said so?

Suddenly a new idea came to Creed. Had Margot

Dalziel been in her nephew's car while he was buying the flowers, but dead? Had he dumped her body in some wood or pond soon afterwards and then somehow, later on, managed to go to the cottage and fake the scene of the struggle there? Some flowers in the room, since she was said to be so fond of them, would have added a touch of verisimilitude. All the same, when could he have done all that? In the dead of night? Not unless his very newly married wife was his accomplice. Well, it wasn't impossible that she was, except that it was a little hard to discover a motive. But still, perhaps it ought to be considered. For if she was not his accomplice, the only time that Roderick had had to himself in the cottage was the minute or two when he had gone in, leaving his wife talking to Miss Hardwicke, and had discovered the disorder inside. And no one could possibly have set that scene in a minute or two.

So was the truth simply that Roderick had bought those roses for his mother-in-law? Were there two bunches of roses in the case?

Creed ground his teeth. Why had he ever thought of that? As if there weren't enough flowers in this case already, chrysanthemums and dahlias, without there having to be two bunches of roses instead of only one. But it was such a simple explanation and really far likelier than any other, and now that he had thought of it he would have to investigate it, would have to question the old Gorgon, would have to lay himself open to the ridicule and criticism which she was certain to heap on him whether he was right or wrong. If he was right, she would jeer at him for not having taken it as a matter of course, if he was wrong, for ever having thought of it. . . .

Wearily, Creed picked up the telephone on his desk and said that he was ready now to see Mr. Dalziel.

Neil Dalziel was brought in by the young man who had been to the Hardwickes' with Creed. At a nod from Creed, he stayed in the room, drawing a chair forward for Dalziel.

" I'm sorry we missed each other earlier," said Creed
as Dalziel sat down, " and very sorry we've no good news
for you of your sister."

" Have you any of any kind? " asked Dalziel. He gave
Creed one long, direct look, as if he were measuring him,
but whether as ally or antagonist it was impossible to tell.
Then he crossed his knees and looked down at the toe of
one foot which began a circling motion in the air.

" Nothing conclusive, I'm afraid," said Creed.

" This horrible affair of the Applin child . . ."

" Yes? " said Creed.

" There can't be any connexion between the two
things, can there? "

" Why do you think there can't? " Creed asked.

" Then *is* there a connexion? "

" There aren't any signs of a sexual assault, if that's
what you want to know," said Creed, " and that, of
course, makes it natural to wonder. . . ." He shrugged
his shoulders.

Dalziel looked up briefly then down again at the restless
movement of his foot. " I see," he said. " Yes. Well,
don't you want to ask me anything, Inspector? I was
there, you know. I was in the cottage when it happened.
That's to say, that's my version of it. But no one I know
of can tell you when I got there."

" That's certainly taking the bull by the horns," said
Creed with a rather bleak smile. He was always cautious
when he encountered people who were determined to
make the cap fit, before you were even sure yourself that
you wanted them to try it on. " Can you explain that a
little more? "

" It's why I came," said Dalziel. " I want to tell you
what I was doing there. I'd had an idea, you see, that
I'd like to take a look at my sister's books. Some are quite
valuable and of course they oughtn't to be left in a place
that's empty half the time. Still, there they are. So it
occurred to me it might be useful to make sure that they
really were there—all of them. I didn't think of trying to

do it secretly, but still, when no one answered when I knocked and I found the door wasn't locked, I wasn't sorry. I went in and started looking over the books. I saw at once that certain ones were missing. Newton's *Method of Fluxion and Infinite Series* and his *Optical Lectures*. There may be others, I don't know. I was doing it by memory and almost at once I was interrupted. First of all, Mrs. Dalziel came in from the garden. But she came in by the back door and stayed in the kitchen, so I didn't draw her attention to the fact that I was in the sitting-room. Then Miss Hardwicke arrived and joined Mrs. Dalziel in the kitchen and the two started having an extraordinarily interesting conversation, so I listened to it, again without drawing their attention to my presence. Mrs. Dalziel suggested it was possible that my sister could have come down to the cottage alone, settled down to a bout of solitary drinking, then started to smash the place up herself, knocking herself out somehow while she was at it, and could then have been found there unconscious by some hypothetical lover, who took her away to his home."

" And do you think there's any likelihood of that being true? " Creed inquired, without revealing any feelings about this suggestion.

" I'm afraid not the very slightest," said Dalziel.

" These books you mentioned," said Creed, " you're certain they aren't there? "

" I'm certain they aren't on the bookshelves in the sitting-room. But I haven't searched the rest of the cottage and I don't know if my sister herself sold them, or lent them, or sent them away somewhere for repair. Still, I thought you ought to know that just possibly they were removed without my sister's knowledge."

" And that she found out about it—yes," said Creed. " That's a very interesting idea. Thank you, Mr. Dalziel. Now would you mind telling me a little more about your movements on Saturday and Sunday? "

On Saturday, Dalziel told him, he had spent the

morning at home in his flat in Chelsea. His housekeeper, he said, would corroborate that. He had met a friend for lunch and they had remained together until about three o'clock. Afterwards he had driven down to see his sister, arriving at the cottage at about five-fifteen. When no one had paid any attention to his ringing, he had waited for some time, then on the advice of Miss Hardwicke, with whom he had spoken in the road, he had gone to look for his sister at the barn. But the barn too had been empty, so he had gone into Fallford for dinner, then returned to the cottage, but had still found it empty.

That had been at about eight-thirty, he thought. He had given up then and gone home. No, he had not seen any firelight in the sitting-room. No, the curtains had not been drawn. He was sure that they had not, because he had tried to look in at the window, and although it had been too dark to see anything in the room, he knew that he had not found himself looking merely at folds of curtain.

On Sunday, he went on, he had tried to telephone the cottage from his home, but had received no answer. Again he had spent the morning at home and he had been at lunch when Roderick had telephoned to ask him if he had seen Margot. He had realised that Roderick was disturbed, but not that anything was seriously amiss, and had tried to reassure him by saying that probably something important connected with her work had come up and that she had simply forgotten all about her appointments with them both. Dalziel had remained at home that afternoon, then had gone out to dinner with some friends, returning home about midnight. His housekeeper, who had spent the evening watching television, had waited up for him to tell him the news of his sister's disappearance.

" And this morning I came down here," he said.

" Going back to that visit of yours to look at your sister's books," said Creed, " where did you leave your car when you went in? "

" In the lane," said Dalziel.

" For any particular reason? "

" Only to be out of the way," said Dalziel. " I thought my nephew might want to take his car out and I didn't want to block the drive."

" That was the only reason? "

" What other could I have had? "

" You might, for instance, have decided beforehand you'd like to approach the cottage unobserved."

" It didn't occur to me."

" And was your nephew's car in the drive when you went in? "

" No, as it happened, it wasn't. He'd gone to the village to do some shopping."

Dalziel stood waiting, but as no more questions came, he went to the door.

" I'm staying here at the Bells until to-morrow," he said. " If there's any news at all of my sister, or if you want to get in touch with me, you'll find me there."

" Thank you," said Creed. " If we hear anything, we'll let you know at once."

He wondered, however, as Dalziel went out, what news of his sister would mean to the man. Himself very self-contained, Creed had never learnt to allow other people much credit for the emotions that they did not express. And it would really be very convenient at the moment if Dalziel's feelings were not too tender. He would fit so neatly into the role of the murderer. He could have picked his sister up in London on Saturday afternoon, after the lunch that he had had with the friend that he had mentioned. He could have driven her to the cottage, gone in with her, killed her and been leaving the cottage when he realised that he had been seen by Rachel Hardwicke. That could have resulted in a change of plan, the bundling of the body into the car, the deliberate draw-ing of Miss Hardwicke's attention to his presence, to the fact that he could not get into the cottage, and then the disposal of the body somewhere else.

As for Bernice Applin, suppose he had found her

nosing around his car, when he had returned to it after going to the cottage to check his sister's books. And suppose she had seemed to be taking an interest in something which was actually completely incriminating, even though she herself, probably, would not have realised it. Such as . . . ? Such as bloodstains. Or some article of clothing. Or even a piece of paper with a florist's name on it. Only Dalziel would hardly have overlooked anything quite so obviously dangerous. But what about, say, a petal from a yellow rose? One yellow petal?

The telephone rang.

It was Gower. " I've picked up some information about Kevin Applin," he said. " One of the boys he was with on Saturday has been doing some talking."

" Good," said Creed. " Has he told you where Applin's got to? "

" No, it's about Saturday," said Gower. " He says it was Applin Miss Dalziel was expecting to visit her."

" *Applin?* " It was a bark of incredulity. Creed had hoped to hear something damaging to Kevin Applin's alibi, not a piece of fantastic nonsense.

" Shakes you, doesn't it? " Gower went on equably. " This boy says he saw the letter she wrote him. Swears to it. But he also swears Applin never went, because he was too drunk. They went to the pictures instead. Shall I bring him along? "

" I suppose so," Creed said reluctantly, realising that Gower believed the boy, for whatever reason. And Gower was good with boys, particularly the boys of his own village, most of whom he had known since their infancy.

Suddenly, as he put the telephone down, Creed had a vision of those yellow roses. Those magnificent roses for Kevin Applin. Was that the kind of woman she was? With all her success and sophistication, her pleasant home and her precious old books, was it that crude chunk of youth and muscle that she wanted when she got home?

For a few minutes Creed completely believed it. Then he decided that the boy whom Gower was bringing in was obviously a liar who merely wanted a little of the notoriety that his friend Kevin acquired so easily. For once Gower must have slipped up.

But then again doubt crept in. These things happened. Every damned thing happened.

When Gower and the boy appeared, the very unwillingness with which the boy told what he claimed to know gave it a certain credibility. There was no glibness about him, no eagerness to make the most of a dramatic story. However, there was not much else about him to inspire trust. He was small, thin and white-faced, with small, suspicious eyes and a slack mouth. A great tuft of dark hair was combed down over his forehead and glistened with oil. He wore a long black jacket and tight trousers. He did not look at all like the farmer's son that he was. His name was Winston Dawes.

Patient questioning by Creed and prompting by Gower made him repeat the story that Gower had already heard. Kevin, said Winston, had had a letter from Miss Dalziel, a letter that had asked him to come and see her on Saturday. He had shown it to Winston and to Ron Wood, the other boy who had been with them on Saturday, while they had been drinking at the White Lion to celebrate Kevin's homecoming. They had all laughed and laughed and then Kevin had suddenly got angry and said what was there to laugh at?

"He said why shouldn't he go if he wanted to," said Winston. "He said he was going to see what he could make out of it. Then he said he wasn't going and acted kind of scared at the idea. Then he said he was going. And he kept on carrying on like that all the time, going and not going, and in the end he reckoned he was too drunk to go anywhere, and we went to the pictures."

"What was in this letter?" asked Creed. "Can you remember?"

"There wasn't nothing much in it," said Winston.

"What did it say?"

" It said he was to come and see her Saturday."

" Just that? She just told him to come and see her? "

" Well, not just *told* him. There was something about her making it worth his while."

" I don't see what there was to laugh at so much in that," said Creed.

" No, dare say there wasn't. It was the way Kev read it." The boy wriggled his thin shoulders. " I told you, we'd been drinking."

" It sounds as if she might just have been asking him to come and do some ordinary little job for her," said Creed.

" No," said Winston. " She made it sound kind of mysterious. Made you wonder what she was getting at. And why'd she have picked on Kev, when she had Mr. Burden to do any job she wanted?"

Creed nodded. " That's a point. Only Mr. Burden may be leaving. Did she ask Applin for any particular time on Saturday? "

" Any time between twelve o'clock and five, she said."

Twelve, thought Creed, when she would have arrived by the train on which she usually travelled, and five, when she expected her brother.

" When did she write this letter? " he asked.

" Dunno," said Winston.

" Well, when did Applin get it? "

" Saturday first thing."

" D'you know where it was posted? "

Winston looked vacant and shook his head, which made the oily lock of hair slip down into his eyes. He thrust it back with a nervous gesture.

" Didn't you see the stamp on it? " Creed asked. " Can't you remember what sort of stamp it was? "

" Stamp? " said Winston. " I dunno. Threepence, I reckon."

" I meant English or foreign."

" Oh. English, most likely. If it'd been foreign Ron

would've looked at it. He likes stamps. I reckon it was English."

But that meant, thought Creed, if there was any truth in what the boy was saying, that almost the first thing that Miss Dalziel had done on arriving back from her important conference in Geneva, was post that letter to Kevin Applin. In fact, she had probably posted it at London Airport, for if she had left it any later than that, she could not have been sure of the letter being delivered on Saturday morning. And that meant that she had written the letter on the plane. And that made it sound a very important letter, just as her haste, when she arrived at the cottage, made it appear that she considered the appointment itself important.

Yet there had been no smoke from the chimney in the morning.

" Are you sure Applin didn't go to see her later, when he'd sobered up? " Creed asked.

" No," said Winston. " After the pictures we had fish and chips."

" And then? "

" Then we all went home."

" Did you see Applin home? "

" Course we didn't."

" Then how d'you know he didn't go to see Miss Dalziel after he'd left you? "

" Because he said he was going home. He said he wasn't feeling too good and he was going home to bed. None of us wasn't feeling too good."

That sounded entirely likely. But an intriguing thought had just come into Creed's head and he sat staring at the boy opposite him with a frown that brought Winston Dawes forward tensely to the edge of his chair.

" It's the truth I'm telling you, Mr. Creed, every word of it! " he protested. " She wrote Kev that letter and she told him to come and see her Saturday."

But it was of Kevin's visit to Browder, the market-gardener, that Creed was thinking at that moment. Suppose

Kevin, his vanity all blown up by receiving Miss Dalziel's letter, and seeing some dahlias in Browder's packing shed, had had an impulse to do things in style and take Miss Dalziel some flowers. Browder would very likely have given him a bunch for nothing, and Kevin could have tied them on to the carrier of his motorbike. But then he had changed his mind about going. So when he reached home in the evening the dahlias would still have been tied to the carrier and Bernice could have helped herself to them, or Kevin might have given them to her, with orders to get some money for them.

If only that were true, that would be one bunch of flowers out of the way!

" If you don't believe me," Winston went on shrilly, " you ask Ron Wood. He'll tell you just the same as me. Or you can ask Mr. Burden."

" Burden? " Creed said quickly.

" That's right," said Winston. " Kev showed him that letter before he went to see Mr. Browder about getting his job back. He stopped at the barn and showed Mr. Burden the letter. Him and Kev always got along all right before Kev got into trouble. Kev always said he was all right. So Kev thought he'd show him the letter and ask him what he thought, him knowing Miss Dalziel and all."

" I see," said Creed, trying not to let the excitement that he suddenly felt sound in his voice. " And what did Mr. Burden say? "

But there Winston fell back on his favourite answer. " Dunno."

Impatiently Creed pressed him, " Did he advise Applin to go or stay away? "

" Dunno," said Winston.

" Come on, come on! " said Creed. " What did Applin tell you about it? "

" He didn't say nothing much," said Winston. " He just started laughing. We all started laughing."

Creed stood up.

" All right," he said, " that'll do for now."

He would soon get out of Burden what he had advised Kevin Applin to do. But first he picked up the telephone again. He rang up Browder. Had Browder, he asked, given Kevin Applin any dahlias on Saturday morning?

" For God's sake! " the market gardener answered. " Dahlias!—I lifted them a fortnight ago. Can't you let that boy alone for a change? You're really out to ruin him, aren't you? "

His face reddening angrily, Creed put the telephone down. Another bright idea that was no good. No good at all.

CHAPTER XIV

MRS. MEREDITH did not stay long with the Hardwickes. As soon as she left, Paul went up to his study. He had a deceptive feeling that what she had said about independence for the young had fired his imagination and that a few telling paragraphs on how not to bring up children would flow from his pen. Sitting down at his desk, he pulled the manuscript of his book towards him and for some minutes deluded himself that he was going to work.

But his thoughts were too tumultuous to take form. Independence, he thought. She talked about independence, that ogreish woman. And all she seemed to understand by it was no cleanliness training. She ought to have a nice chat about that with Mrs. Applin, her sister under the skin. A sudden vision came to Paul, full of pity, of that queer little girl Jane as a poor, wet, smelly baby, having the meaning of all her actions continuously explained to her in that dreadful voice.

But thinking of Jane reminded Paul of Rachel, and that brought him sharply up against the fact that his main reason for rushing up here had been to escape the sight of Rachel's face as she took in the fact that that wretched man on whom she had set her heart had both known Jane Meredith well and kept it a secret. Rachel's face always gave away everything that she felt, at least to anyone who knew her well, and a terror that she might realise that her father had seen the startled humiliation in her eyes had sent Paul headlong out of the room.

He had no idea what he really ought to have done. Ought he to have stayed and tried to cheer her up with some bright remarks about the virtue of finding things out before it was too late? Alternatively, about the actual unimportance of the matter? But wasn't its importance or unimportance just what she had to decide for herself? She was a little past the wet, smelly stage, when some help with the problems of life was really necessary. She was past thirty. And so often, Paul thought, when he tried to help her, his advice somehow only brought about what was best for himself. So hadn't his running away perhaps had a sound instinct behind it, even if cowardice had been dominant for the moment?

Downstairs Rachel had temporarily forgotten his existence. She was licking her wound and trying to convince herself that it did not hurt. She was finding plenty of sensible reasons for deciding that there had never been any need for Brian to tell anyone that it had been Jane who had introduced him to Margot Dalziel, that it had been Jane who had persuaded Miss Dalziel to let him live in the barn. And now at least the puzzling way that Brian had stayed out of sight once Jane had appeared on the scene had a fairly obvious explanation. He had simply been licking a grievous wound of his own in the privacy of the barn.

But Rachel wanted intensely to see him. For one thing, she wanted to warn him that Mrs. Meredith had picked on him as the murderer. For another, she wanted to make some crucial test of her own feelings. She wanted to be near him again and find out what it did to her. Fetching her coat and hoping that her father would not hear her, she slipped quietly out by the back door into the garden.

She went to the bottom of the garden and climbed through the broken gap in the wall. The evening was very dark, with the cruel wind still in possession, making the invisible trees sigh and groan around her. It would have been far easier to go round by the road, but the thought of the spot in the lane where her father had found Bernice sent Rachel slipping and stumbling along the edge of the field, and blundering her way, with torn stockings, through the brambles of the orchard.

There was a light in the window of the barn. Making her way round the old building, she knocked at the door. She had been rather afraid of the moment when Brian would open it, yet when he did, she found herself unexpectedly calm. It was the sort of calm that lasts for a time after a struggle that has ended in surrender. The surrender in this case was to the understanding of him that she had really had all along, to her knowledge that she was no part of his life and never would be.

She saw that she was not even the person whom he had been expecting when he opened the door, but he stood there passively, waiting for her to speak, until she said, " May I come in? "

" I'm sorry," he said, stepping aside to let her in.

There was a lassitude in his big body which gave his movements the quality of a slow-motion film. Rachel went towards the stove, but as she came close to it, realised that it gave off hardly any heat.

" I'm sorry," Brian mumbled again, lifting the top off it and looking inside. " I'm afraid I forgot it and the damned thing's gone out. It always goes out if you don't keep fussing over it."

" Aren't you cold? " she asked. She thought that he looked both cold and tired.

" I think I was just beginning to realise I was, but I was busy." He gestured at the litter of papers on the table. " I suppose it sounds quite hard-hearted to be working on a day like this, but I thought that if I'm going to be turned out soon, I'd better get on."

Rachel remembered Mrs. Meredith's description of him as a big, grubby sort of young man who pretended to write books, and thought that although he was certainly big, and quite often grubby, there was certainly no pretence about the writing. There was an enormous quantity of typescript on the table.

" Are you sure you're going to be turned out? " she asked.

" I should think so," he said. " If Margot turns up, she'll want the place for Jane and Roderick. If she doesn't, I suppose they'll sell it and the cottage as soon as they can. And even if they don't, they aren't going to want to have me living here."

" We've just had a visit from Mrs. Meredith," said Rachel. " She came over to collect Jane and Roderick and take them home with her."

" Oh," said Brian vaguely.

" Brian, what an awful woman she is! "

" Yes, she is rather," he agreed.

" I understand Jane falling in love with Miss Dalziel, if that's what her mother's like."

" I suppose so."

Neither of them had sat down, but had remained standing with the cooling stove between them. Rachel had an impulse to go on chattering, hoping that sooner or later Brian would take it into his head to start talking to her about Jane.

" Mrs. Meredith doesn't like you much, does she? " she said.

" Doesn't she? " he said without any sound of interest.

" Brian, she's made up her mind that you're at the bottom of everything that's been happening."

" Has she? " he said.

" Yes, she has," said Rachel.

" Oh well," he said.

She searched his face for a moment, then said, " Brian, do you understand what I said? "

He seemed to try to rouse himself out of his indifference. " Oh yes, of course," he said. " The old woman doesn't like me. Thinks I'm a murderer. It's amusing in a way, because I used sometimes to think that what she had against me was that I wasn't delinquent enough to be interesting."

" But she said she knew some things about you which she was going to tell the Chief Constable, so perhaps she thinks you are delinquent."

" Oh well, good luck to her," he said. " Thanks for the warning."

She could not tell if the information worried him or not. His slowness and vagueness were at all times a wonderful mask.

" Is your book nearly finished? " she asked.

" Which one? " he asked.

" The one you've been working on all this time," she said.

" Oh." He pushed his fingers through his untidy hair. " Of course, I was forgetting . . . I've been writing several, and the first two have been accepted, and the third's being read at the moment and then there's this one." He nodded at the heap on the table. " And there's one I've got more or less worked out, but I've only the rough plan of it written down. Didn't I ever tell you about all that? "

" You haven't actually told me very much about anything," she said.

His tired eyes concentrated on her face for a moment, then he looked down.

" No, I remember," he said. " You seemed to be like Margot, expecting great things of me. It always embarrassed me, so I kept off the subject as much as I could. I'm just extremely prolific, you see, and hoping to be able to live by that, if I'm lucky. Adventure,

154

romance, mystery, what have you—put me in front of a typewriter and it trickles on and on like a tap with a leaky washer. The speed's limited by my typing. When I can afford to buy a dictaphone, I shall get on better."

Rachel wanted to laugh. She was half-inclined not to believe him, because she found it so difficult to imagine him working fast, thinking fast, doing anything fast. But he seemed quite serious.

" And Miss Dalziel didn't know that? " she asked.

" No," he said. " That was Jane's idea. She thought Margot would feel more inclined to patronise a literary sort of writer than someone like me. I don't know if she was right. Once I got to know Margot a little, I thought all she worried about was the garden, and how well I looked after it. Which was a reasonable viewpoint, I thought, and I generally tried to do my best for her. But Jane may have been right about her. She's got an odd, fey sort of shrewdness. Nothing about anyone ever seems to surprise her. She never starts off by assuming it's impossible that someone else should feel or do something a bit unexpected. She takes anything that comes as a matter of course, and generally thinks it's wonderful as well, so long as it's quite different from the way her family does things. In effect, she's quite unshockable, and that means she sometimes sees things that most of us miss."

" But didn't Miss Dalziel ever want to see anything you'd written? " said Rachel. " Did she go entirely by what Jane told her? "

" Oh, I showed her a few bits and pieces, of course." As he said it a dull flush spread over his face. " She didn't really know the difference."

And he meant, Rachel suddenly knew, the difference between his own work and somebody else's.

As soon as she had thought it, she felt scared. She felt as if the idea could not possibly have been her own, as if by herself she could never have dreamt of such a thing, that it had come from some malign influence that was in the air around them at the moment and that for her to have any peace of mind, it had better be immediately and sharply rejected.

But Jane, if Brian was right about her, would probably not have rejected it, would not even have been much distressed. And Brian would have loved her for it. He had once said that Roderick had married her because she was the one woman he had met who didn't frighten him. But what he had really meant, thought Rachel, was that she was the one woman he had never been frightened of himself.

" Brian, why did Jane marry Roderick instead of you? " she asked.

He shrugged his shoulders. " Impatience, perhaps. Or perhaps you hit on it when you said it was Margot she really fell in love with. Or perhaps it was just because he was on the spot. She's very easily pushed into anything by whoever happens to be there. And I only saw her at week-ends—some week-ends."

" And that's what Kevin meant when he said he thought you were alone because there wasn't a car here."

The flush that had been fading darkened again. " Yes, I suppose so."

" He knew about her coming."

" Yes. And Roderick didn't, you see. Still doesn't. I saw her for a few minutes alone this afternoon and she told me so. And if that's how she wants it, it seems best to leave it like that, doesn't it? "

" When did she let you know about her marriage? " Rachel asked.

" When she drove over to see me on Saturday morning . . ." He stopped. He gave his forehead a blow with his knuckles. " I didn't mean to say that to anyone. I got Kevin to promise he'd say nothing about it as long as I—as I tried to help him if he got mixed up in trouble over Margot's disappearance. He said whatever had really happened, they were bound to go after him." He moved closer to Rachel and gripped her arm. " You won't say anything about it either, will you? Jane's coming here on Saturday can't have had anything to do with what happened to Margot, but she's lied to the police about it, which was damned silly, but it's too late to change it now, and if they get on to it, they'll question her and then it'll get to Roderick."

Rachel felt as if her real self had gone a long way away. Either it or the other self that was here was feeling very sorry for someone, but she was not sure who it was. It might have been Brian, or it might have been Roderick, or it might even have been Jane, because, of course, you had to remember that mother of hers and make allowances. Oddly enough, it did not seem to be for herself.

" All right, Brian," she said, " I won't talk about it. But how did Kevin think you could help him? "

" Mostly by keeping quiet about a letter he'd had from Margot, asking him to go and see her on Saturday. He showed it to me, to ask if I thought he ought to go or not. I told him to do whichever he liked. Then next day he came round to tell me he hadn't been. That was when you saw him."

She drew her arm out of his grasp. " It was *Kevin* she was expecting? But why?"

" He assumed it was for the sake of his charm," said Brian, " but somehow I doubt it, in spite of the roses and the drinks."

Outside Rachel heard a car stop and then voices.

" I think that's the police," she said.

She saw Brian close his eyes for a moment and she thought he gave a shudder.

" All right," he said. " But that means you'd better go."

" I'll go as soon as I can," she said. " It won't help if I try to dash away now."

" But you'll remember . . . ."

With an explosion of anger that she could not control, she said in a furious whisper, " I promised, didn't I? "

A knock sounded on the door. Brian went towards it. Just before he opened it he gave one look into Rachel's face and she saw the curious, half-guilty perception that she had sometimes seen in his eyes before, as if he were really very sorry that he knew as much about her as he did and hoped that his knowledge did not hurt her. He opened the door.

Creed and Gower stood side by side in the darkness outside. Creed began to say something, saw Rachel and hesitated.

" I'm just leaving," she said, " unless you want me."

" No, I just wanted a few words with Mr. Burden," said Creed. " But are you going home alone? "

" Oh yes." She thought that he was wondering if he ought to send Gower to see her safely home, but at that moment she wanted nobody's company but her own. " I'll go through the orchard into our garden," she said. " It takes about two minutes. Good night, Brian."

" Good night," he said.

She went out, passing the two policemen on the threshold.

As they went in and the door was shut after them, it cut off the shaft of light that had lain across the path, and until her eyes began to get used to the dark, Rachel found herself in sudden complete blackness. It was only then that she realised that there was silence too. While she had been talking to Brian, the wind had died. Only a faint rustling came from the trees, as if at last the strained branches were wearily settling themselves.

Although she had shuddered at the gale all day, Rachel found something eerie in the quiet. It seemed too like the emptiness in her own heart. She went forward slowly, picking her way among the brambles, and sometimes standing still and thinking, almost forgetting where she was.

The difficult thing to take in was that all this time that she had known Brian, the image of him that had filled her thoughts had been the merest shadow. Her intuitions had told her nothing about any of the things that were most important to him. His face, his slow voice, his big, passive body had made up the whole of him. And, of course, the fact that he was there, and alone, when she happened to be there and virtually alone too. She had acted as if she were sixteen instead of going to be thirty-four in December. She had never guessed at Jane's existence, or tried to understand what sort of work he was really doing, or dreamt that he was capable of deliberately deceiving Margot Dalziel about it. And how much more was there that she did not know?

The fact that there must be a great deal seemed to her to be entirely her own fault. She would almost have liked to apologise to him for it. What an embarrassment he must have found her obvious and blind love. Yet on the whole he had been sensitive about it and spared her what he could.

A twig cracked in the darkness near her.

She started. She was not sure that there had really been a sound. She had been lost in herself, hardly remembering where she was, although by now she could see the shapes of the quiet trees around her. If there had been a sound, she thought, it had probably been something falling to the ground out of the battered branches, or perhaps a bird had been scratching amongst the dead leaves. Yet in spite of thinking this, she felt all at once that it would be a good thing to hurry. She took a few blundering steps onward, then stopped again. She was certain now that her own footsteps had not been the only ones that she had heard.

Yet when she stood still there were no sounds near her but the faint whispering of leaf against leaf. Pushing at some drooping branches in her way, she went on.

This time she heard the other footsteps clearly. They were behind her and nearer than that first cracking of a twig. Panic made her helpless for an instant, then all of a sudden she started to run. She reached the gap in the hedge, plunged through it and ran on, along the edge of the field, turning her ankle in a rough furrow and feeling pain tear at her muscles, but thinking of the gap in the garden wall as safety.

He caught her just before she reached it. An arm came round her from behind, wrenching her backwards, and a hand came over her mouth. She tried to scream and to twist away from the breath on her neck and the hard-muscled body behind her, then she tried to bite and was given a blow on the side of the head for it.

" Quiet, now! Try that again and I'll do worse," said the adenoidal voice of Kevin Applin. " Keep quiet and you won't get hurt. What was he telling you? "

It took him a moment to realise that she could not answer. He moved his hand from her mouth but took a grip of her arm above the elbow, digging his fingers into the flesh.

" I was watching you," he said. " I heard some of it. You was talking about me. What did he tell you? "

" Let me go! " she sobbed wildly. " He didn't tell me anything. Let me go! "

" That's a lie. You was talking about me," he said.

" Where've you been? " she asked. " The police are looking for you."

He swore with dull vindictiveness at the police and also at her and her stupidity, if she thought that they would ever look for anyone else. His fingers dug again. " What did he tell you? Something about that letter, wasn't it? I heard him."

" If you heard him, what are you asking me for? " she cried.

" That letter's nothing, I never went," he said.

" That's what he told me."

" That's a lie, he told you I went, didn't he? Didn't he? "

" He didn't, but what does it matter what he told me? "

" Creed's in there now. Is he going to tell Creed I went? "

" I don't know. It won't hurt you much if you didn't. You ought to have told Creed all about it yourself."

He repeated his former unimaginative curses, the formula he used for expressing all anger, all fear.

" I never went near her and I never laid a hand on Bernice. Me! " His voice suddenly quavered and his grip on Rachel's arm loosened. " Me lay a hand on the kid! "

Rachel moved a step away from him.

" I never thought you did," she said.

" I'd gone looking for a job in Portsmouth, but I come home soon as I heard it," he said. " I come home and talked to Dad. He told me about your Dad and the kids. ' They'll never believe it, people won't,' he said, ' but I know what he done,' he said, ' the kids told me.' And I know too. He's always tried to get at the kids and it's only the way they've been brought up, they know better than to listen to him. But Bernice was different. She thought she knew all there was to know. She'd go with anyone."

" Kevin! " Rachel exclaimed. It was too dark for her to see more of his face than a pale blur, but she could see the swaying movement of his head from side to side, the movement of a young bull preparing to charge. " What are you talking about? "

He did not seem to hear her. The dull urgency of his voice as he talked on faster started her heart racing so hard that she could hardly breathe.

" I'll go and settle with him," he said. " I said so to my dad. ' I'll settle with him,' I said. ' People'll believe it then.' But then I see you going in to Burden's, so I stopped and listened and I hear him telling you about the letter. And that made me mad and I near as anything forgot why I come out. But the letter's nothing. It don't matter. He can tell them what he likes. You're going to take me in with you now and I'm going to settle things the way they should be. You needn't get hurt if you do what I say."

He reached for her arm again.

She leapt away to the wall and his hand missed her. She reached the jagged gap in the stonework and almost believed that there was hope of scrambling through it before he caught her again. Yet at the same time she saw herself moving so slowly compared with Kevin that it was as if she were standing still, held fast by him before he touched her.

The moment that he caught her she began to scream. If only she screamed loud enough, it seemed to her, her father might hear her and be warned of Kevin's coming. Yet the terrible thing was that she could not tell if her screams were rending the night or were only little hopeless sobs inside her head. She did not even know how often she screamed before Kevin struck her again. As she fell, he jumped the wall and went running towards the house.

CHAPTER XV

RACHEL PICKED herself up slowly. The darkness was spinning and she felt a certain surprise when she found that her arms and legs were ready to do what she told them. She was more numbed than hurt, except for the pain in the ankle that she had twisted in running. Limping to the wall, she leant against it, listening to her loud, uneven breathing.

It was as she started to climb the wall that she heard noise from the house. There was shouting, then the back door was flung open and Kevin came running out. She saw him clearly against the light that streamed out from the door, then he vanished into the darkness of the garden.

But there was no sound of running footsteps coming towards her. He made for the road. Sick with fear of what she would find in the house, Rachel got down from the wall and had taken her first limping steps towards the door when two figures appeared in the lighted opening and she saw that one was her father.

She called out to him. He stood rigid, uncertain where the call had come from, then came running towards her.

The other man followed him. It was Neil Dalziel. He was panting and mopping at his mouth with a handkerchief.

Paul put his arms round Rachel and held her tightly. He began to scold her.

" I told you—didn't I tell you?—you weren't to rush out without telling me where you were going! I've been going mad with worry since I found out you weren't at home. Where did you go? Are you all right? Why did you go? " It poured out of him, a release for what he had just gone through himself. Then at the first step that they took towards the house, he exclaimed, " Oh, you're hurt! "

" I've twisted my ankle," she said. " It's nothing much. What did Kevin do? "

" Knocked and got inside before I could stop him," said Paul, " and told me he was going to do something he called settling with me. Luckily for me, he wasted time telling me so and Mr. Dalziel was there." He turned to Neil Dalziel. " I haven't thanked you. I don't like to think what would have happened if you hadn't come. . . ."

Dalziel interrupted him. " We ought to telephone the police."

" Yes, yes," said Paul, " of course. At once." But he kept his arm round Rachel until they reached the house and returned to his scolding of her, demanding where she had been.

" I went to tell Brian about Mrs. Meredith," she said.

" You ought to have told me. You oughtn't to have gone out alone. I'd have come with you."

Dalziel had not waited for Paul to finish, but had gone ahead and when Paul and Rachel came through the kitchen into the hall, was already at the telephone. In the light Rachel saw that there was red on the handkerchief that he was holding against the side of his mouth.

She also saw her own face in a mirror on the wall. It was white and one cheek had begun to swell. She touched the cheek gingerly and found it tender but not really painful. But the state of her hand startled her. In her fall the skin had been scraped down the side of it and was smeared with earth, coloured by a slight oozing of blood.

Paul had run upstairs for disinfectant and dressings and was calling to her to go and sit down and that he would come in a moment and attend to her hurts. Dalziel put the telephone down and looked into the mirror over Rachel's shoulder.

" Mirror, mirror on the wall, which is the bloodiest of all? " he inquired, meeting Rachel's eyes in the mirror and smiling with one side of his mouth, while he dabbed at the other with the handkerchief.

She smiled back, equally lop-sidedly. " Anyway, we came out of it safely."

" So did Kevin, I'm afraid."

" I'm glad," she said. " I'm glad he isn't here still."

" The only thing is . . ." Dalziel began, but changed his mind about how to go on. " Oh well, the police should be able to pick him up now."

" The only thing is, he may be back," Rachel finished his first sentence for him.

" Don't worry," he reassured her again. " The police will take care of that."

" He really believed my father had something to do with that child's death," she said, her amazement returning.

Paul came downstairs again with the first-aid box. " And probably half the rest of the village do too by now— Paul Hardwicke, the human monster," he said, trying to make a joke of it, but producing a very shaky attempt at amusement. " Now come along and let me see to those grazes. You too, Mr. Dalziel. As the intended victim, I feel rather bad about being the only one who got off quite scatheless, but at least I can look after you and supply you with drinks—if that's the right thing to do. I always have an uncomfortable feeling that in this sort of situation one's supposed to give the patient tea, but I know what I'd say myself if anyone did that when there was a bottle of whisky in the house." He chattered on, trying to master his own nerves while he administered first aid to them both in the kitchen.

Afterwards they returned to the sitting-room and he produced the whisky.

"At least this clears the air to some extent," he said. "That boy's violence was motivated by a ghastly sincerity, and if he thinks I murdered his sister, then he didn't do it himself. And so probably he didn't have anything to do with Miss Dalziel's disappearance either. Incidentally, how fortunate for me he hasn't graduated to carrying a gun yet. Let's hope he doesn't know where to lay hands on one."

Again his attempt at cheerfulness was a failure, partly because he caught Neil Dalziel's eye as he spoke. Its gaze was uncomfortably sombre.

"Let's hope he doesn't," said Dalziel, "but I wonder if it's wise to take it for granted."

"Oh come," said Paul. "A gun—a gun in this village!"

"Hasn't Fallford got its own underworld?" asked Dalziel. "Most places have nowadays. I don't want to be an alarmist, but I don't think you should go out until they've laid hands on that boy, or open the door either until you're sure who's on the other side of it."

"Ah, I'm with you there. The doors shall be kept bolted and no one shall get in without giving the pass-word," said Paul.

"Seriously," said Dalziel.

"Yes," said Paul soberly. "Quite seriously."

As if to make an immediate test of his seriousness, the door-bell rang. Putting down his drink Paul got up automatically and started for the door.

"Daddy!" Rachel shouted at him.

" It'll be the police," he said.

" You don't know it's the police! "

" Oh," he said, hesitating. " No. Well, I'll make them talk through the letter-box before I open the door. Of course, if they'd bang on the door and shout ' Open up— it's the law! ' it would be quite simple, but I can't imagine Gower doing that."

He went out.

Neil Dalziel followed him, then with a firm hand on Paul's shoulder when he was not expecting it, thrust him to one side and reached the door first himself.

Outside it someone was talking. The voice was neither Gower's nor Creed's, but hearing it Dalziel looked back at Paul with a smile and opened the door.

" Oh, *you're* here! " Jane exclaimed in surprise, breaking off in the middle of what she had been saying to Roderick.

She was holding Roderick's arm. Standing close together, with both their faces white and strained, they made Paul think that they could not possibly be man and wife, but were only a pair of children, playing the game of mothers and fathers, real babes in the wood, more lost than they knew.

" May we come in? " she asked. " An awful thing's happened."

" Yes, come in, of course," said Paul as Dalziel stood aside. " What is it? I thought you were going home to your mother, Jane."

" Home? " she said in a horrified tone. " That would have been the last straw, the very last. Mummy was very put out, of course, but Roderick dealt with her. He's simply wonderful at dealing with Mummy. He said it was our duty to wait in the cottage in case Margot came back. It's always a good thing to get the word duty in before Mummy can herself, and Roderick seemed to know that by instinct. And he was very dignified about it. He made a terrific impression. But that's got nothing to do with it. It's Brian, Mr. Hardwicke. They've arrested him."

" We don't know that they've arrested him," Roderick said quickly. " We just saw him go by in a police car with the inspector."

" But that means they've arrested him! " she cried. " What would Brian be doing in a police car with an inspector if he hadn't been arrested? "

" Perhaps just being questioned," said Paul, thinking of Rachel in the sitting-room and of reassuring her as much as Jane. " But come in to the fire and tell us all about it."

Roderick and Jane came in and went on standing side by side in their defensive partnership against the world.

" We'd decided to go out for a drink, you see," said Jane. " The place was getting on our nerves, so we were going to the Waggoners when the police car came whizzing out of the lane, and there was Brian in it and he saw us but he wouldn't look at us. So I said to Roderick we must go straight to the Hardwickes, because perhaps Mr. Hardwicke can tell us what we ought to do."

" There's nothing we can do," said Roderick. " I keep telling you so."

" But there must be! " she wailed. " Poor Brian. Darling Brian. Mr. Hardwicke, there *is* something we can do, isn't there? "

" I don't know, Jane," said Paul. " I'll try to think of something. If he's really been arrested. But what have they got against him? "

" The books, of course! " she cried. " They must have found out about them somehow—found the pawn-tickets, or something."

" Jane! " Roderick gripped her arm and swung her round to face him. " What books are you talking about? "

" *The* books—you know—the ones that are missing," she said.

All colour drained out of his face. " No, I don't," he said.

" Those ones Neil told you were missing," she said.

Roderick gave Neil Dalziel a glance, then looked back at Jane, then let her arm go and drew a little away from her. In a voice that sounded far too calm, he said, " Did Brian steal them? "

" Of course he did," she said. " Who else possibly could have? I don't mean he *stole* them. But he couldn't actually live on air, could he, poor darling, even in that barn and even if I helped a little? So he borrowed one or two books, to raise some money, just till he started to get some money for his writing. The awful thing about writing, you see, is that you seem to have to wait for nearly ever till you get something actually paid to you. Anyway, the books were perfectly safe, and Margot could have got them back herself any time she liked, if she'd really needed them. But as a matter of fact——" Jane looked round. She seemed unaware of the silence that had fallen in the room. " I'm sure she never even missed them.".

" That's where you're wrong," said Roderick, still in that unnaturally level voice. " She missed them."

Dalziel started. " Roderick, how do you know that? "

But Roderick could only see Jane. " And you knew," he said.

She raised her delicate little claw-like hands and let them fall again in a gesture that admitted everything.

" And I——" He spaced the words far apart, as if he were tasting the bitterness of each in turn. " I—never—realised—anything."

" But he had to do something, hadn't he? " she said. " What would have been the good of giving up everything to start writing and then have to give that up before he'd got anywhere at all? He had a little money to live on at first, of course, but it didn't last long."

" Didn't he think of explaining that to Margot? " Roderick asked.

" He did, as a matter of fact," said Jane. " Only I thought she might be angry."

" You've always said Margot's never angry."

" But I've never tried asking her for money, have I? Sometimes the very nicest people are perfectly horrid if you ask them for money. But I thought if she found out about the books, we could count on her being understanding. She was wonderful about understanding people who succumbed to ungovernable temptations."

" I see," said Roderick. " So you advised Brian to pawn some of her books. It was your idea, wasn't it? "

She gave him a queer little smile, rather as if she were pleased with herself.

" Well, yes," she said. She glanced at Neil Dalziel. " Of course it gave me an awful shock this morning when I saw you looking at the book-case. That's why I dropped that vase."

" And I—never realised——" Roderick began to tremble all over. He sat down suddenly, let his head fall forward and pounded his temples with his fists.

" But there's nothing so very awful about it, is there? " she asked. " I told you the books were quite safe."

He might not have heard her. The pounding went on.

She watched him with bewildered distress. " After all," she said, " you told me yourself how you got a lot of extra expenses out of that travel agency you worked for, so that you could save your salary and have something for us to get married on."

" The books," he muttered, " Margot's books. And Brian! "

She went a step closer to him, then went rigid as he shrank away from her.

" Do try to understand, darling," she pleaded.

He stopped trying to knock himself unconscious, but still kept his head down and pressed his hands flat against his temples.

" I hardly realised you knew Brian at all," he said. " At all well. You hardly ever spoke about him."

" Oh, is *that* what's worrying you? " she said, as if this were a most strange and interesting thing to discover. " It really needn't. Everything's absolutely over between us. It has been for ages. Everything in the least important. If it hadn't been, I'd have told you about it."

At last he raised his head and looked at her. " What a liar you are, Jane! I've often realised you lied to other people, but I never thought you'd lie to me."

" But it wasn't *lying*," she said defensively in a voice that had begun to shake. Her features suddenly crumpled. " I hate being questioned! " she shrieked at him. " I can't stand it! It's like being at home! "

Her explosion seemed to give Roderick back control of himself. " Perhaps it's where you ought to be," he said.

She looked as if he had struck her. Her features went slack and she swayed. Then, saying something in a high, chattering voice, the only distinguishable word of which was " Mummy ! " she turned and bolted from the room.

As the door banged after her, Neil Dalziel said, " For God's sake, Roderick, you can't let her go like that. Go after her! "

Roderick slumped wearily in his chair. " Those books," he muttered to himself.

" Forget the damned books! " said Dalziel. " You can't send her away like that. You've both been behaving like two children in a tantrum."

" Isn't it what we are? " Roderick gave a dull sigh. He looked up at his uncle. " You thought I was the person who stole them, didn't you, Neil? "

" I did, as a matter of fact," said Dalziel. " I was puzzled how you'd got the money to get married on. I didn't think of an expense account. Now for God's sake go and look after your wife. Young Applin's around somewhere in a murderous mood."

" Good heavens, yes! " Paul exclaimed, dragging his thoughts back from an odd little excursion on which they had just started. " We can't leave her alone now. I'll go, shall I? "

" Roderick should go," said Dalziel.

" No, I'll go," said Paul, making up his mind. " I think, after all, that might be best."

" In that case," said Rachel, " I'm coming with you."

She stood up swiftly, forgetting her twisted ankle. The pain made her wince, but she found that if she put her weight carefully on to her foot, she could manage fairly well. Limping after Paul, she called to him to wait for her.

He paused at the front door, saying, " No, Rachel, go back. I can manage best alone."

" I want to talk to you," she whispered. " And we may as well leave those two to each other. Let's go together."

" But your foot," he said.

" I can get as far as the cottage, anyway, if that's where Jane went," she said and took his arm.

Paul gave in and they went through the gate and started walking along the road to Margot Dalziel's cottage.

" Well, what did you want to talk about? " Paul asked.

" It's about what happened when I went to see Brian," she said. " I promised him I wouldn't tell the police and I suppose that meant I wouldn't tell anyone else either, but now it's all come out by itself."

" It's about Jane and Brian? "

" Yes."

" I see," he said. " I was wondering—well, why that scene didn't seem to surprise you."

" And there was something about Kevin, but there was nothing about the books."

As she said it, headlights cut across the road ahead of them. A car came swerving out of the cottage gate, swung to the right and came driving straight down the middle of the road towards them. It was Roderick's car and Jane was at the wheel. If she saw them as they sprang back into the hedge, she gave no sign, but drove straight on, accelerating fast.

" So that's that," said Paul. " She really is going back to Mummy. We may as well go home again."

" Only let me tell you about Kevin and Miss Dalziel's letter," said Rachel. " We may not have much chance to talk after we go in."

" Why, d'you suppose those two are going to stay all night? " Paul asked.

" Well, with Kevin Applin on the prowl, convinced you're a homicidal maniac, I shan't mind if they do. Anyway, we can't turn them out, can we? "

" I can and I will, if I feel like it," said Paul irritably. " Now tell me about this letter. What letter? "

" It's a letter Miss Dalziel wrote to Kevin, asking him to come and see her on Saturday." She felt Paul's start of surprise as she leant on his arm. " Yes really," she said. " Kevin showed the letter to Brian and asked him what he thought he ought to do. I don't think Brian gave him any special advice, but next day Kevin came in to tell him that he hadn't gone to see her—I was there when he arrived— and he got Brian to promise not to tell anyone about the letter by threatening to tell about Jane's visits if he did."

" Miss Dalziel wrote asking Kevin ... It was Kevin she was expecting?" Paul's thoughts went on another disconcerting excursion, but he jerked them back to reality. " Of course it's quite obvious why she wrote to him. Kevin was just out of prison and that made him just her meat— for an article, I mean. The effects of prison on the young criminal—that sort of thing."

Rachel agreed. " But Kevin says he never went to see her. And we said just now he couldn't have killed his sister."

" Yes, yes, that's right. So what are you trying to tell me? "

They had reached the gate and were standing still, talking in lowered voices.

" It's just an idea I had," said Rachel, " after hearing about those books. Jane came to see Brian on Saturday morning and told him about her marriage. She came by car—I suppose her parents' car—I heard Kevin talk about it. Well then, suppose she went in to see Miss Dalziel afterwards, perhaps taking her the roses and having a drink with her. And then suppose Miss Dalziel told her she knew about her taking the books and—and suppose Jane lost her head."

" It's a head that certainly isn't screwed on too tightly," said Paul thoughtfully. " But is she strong enough to have moved the body afterwards? She's such a thin little bit of a girl. My dear, if you're right, I'm afraid what you'd have to face is that Brian moved the body."

He felt her shudder as she leant against him. " I can't imagine him hurting a fly. And Miss Dalziel was so small and light. I really think Jane might have been able to move her alone. And this afternoon, when Bernice left you and went running down the lane, Jane was in the garden. She'd been out picking some leaves to put in a vase. If she knew that Bernice had seen her on Saturday and then heard that scream. . . ."

" But Miss Dalziel was pleased about Roderick's marriage to Jane," said Paul. " Would she have been pleased if she'd known about the books? "

" It was on Friday evening that she was pleased," said Rachel.

" Yes, so it was. You mean she might only have found out the books were missing when she got home on Saturday—perhaps only a few minutes before Jane showed up. . . ."

A sound distracted him. It was the sound of a motor cycle, coming from the direction of the village. The noise of it had already been in his ears for a moment, but it was only when he remembered Neil Dalziel's call to the police and that Sergeant Gower often used a motor cycle, that its roar broke into his thoughts.

Paul had no desire just then to be kept talking by a policeman. Some things that had been said in that scene between Jane and Roderick had gone on stirring in his mind and he had only just realised what he wanted to do about it.

" Quick—inside ! " he said and thrust Rachel towards the door. " And stay there. And whatever you do, don't open the door till you know who wants to come in."

Rachel swung round in the doorway, only realising when the door was half-closed behind her that Paul was not following her in.

" What are you doing? Where are you going? " she cried.

" Never mind, I shan't be long," he said.

" Are you going to the barn? "

" Yes, yes, to the barn."

It was a lie. He had not even thought of going to the barn. But he did not want to be stopped again. Pulling the door shut he went running down the garden to the gap in the wall and was clambering through it as the motor cycle roared up to the door.

Paul had quite forgotten that Kevin Applin rode a motor cycle.

CHAPTER XVI

PAUL's real destination was the Applins' home and naturally he was expecting difficulties. For one thing, he realised, he might encounter Kevin and although Paul had remembered to bring his stick, the meeting was likely to be very unpleasant. For another thing, the Applins might refuse to let him in. For a third, anyone who took it on himself to try to extract some sense from those two inarticulate humans, Myrna and Loraine, which was Paul's aim at the moment, was in for trouble.

So, all considered, things did not turn out too badly. Mrs. Applin, in her heavy and silent way, was unexpectedly welcoming, while her husband, who had drunk himself past the quarrelsome stage into a groaning stupor, lay on the bed and took no interest in what was happening. Nobody spoke of Kevin. A motor cyclist's helmet lay on a chair and seeing it, Paul had a feeling that it ought to tell him something, but he was so relieved at finding that he had no need to nerve himself to deal with Kevin that he forgot all about the motorcycle that he had heard coming when he left home. In any case, he still assumed that it belonged to Gower.

To his surprise, Paul found that Mrs. Applin wanted the two young children to talk to him. They'd got to talk to somebody, she said. She had tried to make them talk to Jim Gower, but they had only cried and acted foolish, in spite of what she had promised to do to them if they didn't speak up. She herself couldn't make out what they meant about the flowers Bernice had picked up in the garden. There was a man in the story and she didn't know if he'd given the flowers to Bernice or what. She was sure Bernice wouldn't ever take flowers if they hadn't been given to her, but then again, if they'd just been thrown away . . . Anyway, she knew the police had been asking questions about some flowers, so the children ought to tell what they knew.

She seemed to have lost her suspicion of Paul and to feel that more help might come to her now from him, from Gower and from those who lived on good terms with the law than from those on whom she relied in more normal circumstances.

With her help, Paul had a fairly successful conversation with Myrna and Loraine. He had one great advantage over Gower. He knew more or less what the children had to tell him. At least, he believed that he did, so he did not scruple to put a good many words into their mouths. Then he only had to watch for the dumb, hesitant nod that confirmed what he had suggested. A half-crown, which their mother allowed them to keep at least until after the visitor had left, seemed to help their mental processes.

" It was on Sunday morning Bernice found the flowers, wasn't it? " he said.

Myrna's head nodded and after a slight pause, Loraine carefully copied her.

" The man came to the door and threw them out? "

Another nod.

" Was it the back door? "

A nod.

" And Bernice picked them up and brought them to my house and sold them to my daughter? "

This brought a rather lengthy and protesting answer from Myrna, which was quite unintelligible to Paul.

Mrs. Applin translated it. " She says he put them in the dust-bin. She says Bernice said it was all right taking them if they was in the dust-bin."

" She saw the man put them there, did she? " Paul asked.

They both nodded.

" Did you see him too? "

They nodded.

" Did you know him? "

They nodded.

" Who was he? "

They both looked blank, then started to cry.

Their mother said, " They don't know his name, you see, Mr. Hardwicke, so it wasn't Mr. Burden. Besides, he always got on all right with the kids and I don't think there's any harm in him. This other man, they've seen him about, so they say they know him, but they don't know who he is."

" Never mind," said Paul. " I know who it was. I just wanted to be sure it was on Sunday morning that Bernice found the flowers. She saw the man put them in the dust-bin by the back door, she took them out and brought them round to my house—that's what happened, isn't it? "

The two dark, tousled heads nodded again.

" And now there's just one more thing I'd like to ask," said Paul. " It's about the milk-bottle that vanished from Miss Dalziel's doorstep. . . ."

He never finished the question, for at the first mention of a milk-bottle Myrna and Loraine ran behind their mother, hid their faces against her and began to scream.

Paul found that as clear an answer as he needed. It was the children who had removed the bottle, not Margot Dalziel or her murderer. She had not come to the cottage on Saturday morning. The truth was that she had never come at all. Paul was sure of that now. He said good-bye to Mrs. Applin and started homeward.

This time he went by the road, walking slowly as he tried to put his thoughts in order. He was sure that he knew who had murdered Margot Dalziel and Bernice Applin. The odd story about the dahlias confirmed it. But what was he to do about it?

He had nothing that could be called proof. He was merely able to put together a consistent story of what must have happened. But a mere story was hardly likely to satisfy the police. It would never make any impression on a cautious, unimaginative man like Creed, who happened not to have been there when Roderick Dalziel had turned on his uncle and accused him of believing that he had stolen the missing books. There had been so extreme a bitterness on Roderick's face at that moment that it could not possibly have come from a single injustice. There had been far more behind it. And that was when it had suddenly occurred to Paul that if Margot Dalziel had believed the same, had charged Roderick with it and refused to accept his denials, he might easily have lost that fierce temper of his, which had shown itself more than once during the last day or two, and turned on her with violence. Far greater violence, perhaps, than he ·even knew he had in him. But it hadn't happened in the cottage, and not on Saturday. . . .

No, of course not. Still, this didn't solve the problem of what Paul was to do about it now.

Unfortunately, he thought, as he picked his way along the muddy lane, he hardly ever seemed to know what to do about anything. He had thought that something ought to be done about the Applin children, he had been willing to do something, but had simply not known what. He had wanted somehow to make Rachel see that Brian was not her kind, but he had only muddled, temporised and left her to find it out for herself. And if that had really been the best thing to do, because nothing but her own experience would ever have meant much to her, it had been by chance. Paul's knowledge of life had not helped her in any way. If he had any.

And now she would want to return to her old job in London and he would have to encourage her, would even have to insist on it, if she pretended to be unwilling to go. And he would have to look for a housekeeper. Oh God, oh God! Of course, if there was anything in an idea that he had had that day that she and Neil Dalziel were more attracted to each other than either realised, there might be no need to hurry her away. Dalziel would have to spend some time in the village in the near future to settle up his sister's affairs and while the trial was pending he and

Rachel were likely to see a good deal of each other. And they would suit each other in many ways. They were both naturally shy people, who would understand, from experience, how to be kind to one another's nervous systems and learn a comforting freedom with one another. . . .

No! Paul slashed viciously with his stick at a stone in the road. No more of this self-deception. She must go back to London, go back to her own work, lead her own life, and that was that. The question he had to settle now was what to do about Roderick.

He did not know yet that Kevin Applin had taken that problem out of his hands.

Even when he reached the house and saw the shattered window with the curtains pulled back and Gower inside, bending over something on the floor, Paul did not take in what had happened. He had expected to find Gower there. What he had not expected was to see Rachel with Neil Dalziel's arms round her, hiding her face against him, as if there were something in the room that she could not bear to look at.

When she heard Paul at the door, she ran to meet him, threw her arms round his neck and clung to him.

" He meant to kill you! " she cried. " He thought he was shooting at you! "

Neil Dalziel had followed Rachel from the room.

" It was the Applin boy again," he said, " with the gun we didn't think he had. We both saw him clearly. And Sergeant Gower saw him, riding off. They're bound to get him."

Paul gently slipped out of Rachel's arms and went to the door of the sitting-room. He looked in. Gower saw him, moved away from Roderick's sprawled body and came to the door.

Closing it behind him, he said, " I'm afraid there's nothing you can do here, Mr. Hardwicke. I've phoned Fallford. I'm waiting for Inspector Creed."

" What happened? " Paul asked.

"Applin came back just after you left," said Dalziel. "He simply smashed the window, pulled the curtain back and fired."

"He must have thought Roderick was you," said Rachel. She had begun to cry quietly, without bothering to dry the tears.

"He shot him through the chest," said Dalziel. "Roderick died almost at once. He said . . ." His voice became unsteady. "He said, ' Why won't you believe me, Margot? ' "

"Just that? " said Paul. "Nothing else? "

"Yes, there was something else," said Dalziel. "Something about ' the water.' Or that's what it sounded like. Perhaps he was asking for some water. He only muttered it and then he died."

"No," said Paul, "I don't think he was asking for water. I think he was telling you where to look for your sister's body. In water—some pond or stream between here and London, where he put her after he'd killed her on Friday evening. And I think Kevin may have known what he was doing when he killed Roderick. Kevin had just been home—I've just been there myself and I saw his helmet there—and I think he'd had a talk with his sisters. From that he could have worked out that Roderick was the man who gave Bernice the dahlias."

"The dahlias? " said Rachel. "What have the dahlias to do with this? "

"I'll tell you presently," said Paul, who felt that he could not face telling the story too often, "when Inspector Creed gets here."

It was upstairs in his study, the only room in the house that seemed not to have been invaded by what had happened during the last few days that he later told the story to Rachel, Neil Dalziel, Creed and Gower. He told them how he had guessed that Margot Dalziel, like her brother, had believed that Roderick had stolen her books and with all her love for him, had refused to accept his denials.

Roderick's body had been taken away and a sergeant from Fallford had driven off to break the news to Jane and her parents. Margot Dalziel's body had not yet been found. That happened early the next day. It was in the Fallford canal, a few miles north of the town. She had been strangled with one of her own nylon stockings.

"I'd always realised there was a curious relationship between the two of them," said Paul. "It seemed to be a mixture of great affection with something on her side that was almost a patronising contempt and on his a sort of shrinking resentment. That would have made a fine breeding-ground for false suspicions. I tried, then, to reconstruct the scene between them on Friday evening, assuming she'd found out the books were missing just before she left for Geneva. She'd have had no time to do anything about the matter then, but while she was away she could have given a good deal of thought to what she meant to do. You may remember Jane saying that Margot was wonderful about understanding people who succumbed to ungovernable temptations and we can be sure she'd have decided to act with great forebearance and in everything for Roderick's own good."

"According to her own lights," her brother muttered.

"To be sure," said Paul. "What more could she do than that? Well then, Roderick met her at the airport on Friday and sprang the news on her of his marriage to Jane Meredith. Immediately, I believe, Miss Dalziel had what she thought was a brilliant idea. She would turn Brian Burden out of the barn and put Jane and Roderick into it. Then she'd be able to keep Roderick under her eye and protect him from this streak of dishonesty that he seemed to have. And in the end, of course, she'd cure him of it. Her delight in his marriage was entirely sincere. She can't have understood Jane very well and simply thought of her as a nice little girl who worshipped her and would always cling to her and be happy to save Roderick from himself on his aunt's instructions."

" Yes, that sounds very like Margot," said Dalziel.

" But Roderick had been thinking of marriage as an escape from his aunt's domination," said Paul. " A little belatedly, he was trying to stand on his own feet. He hadn't thought that he was walking into a trap which she was about to close on him."

Dalziel shook his head. " I don't understand. One thing you can be sure of is that Margot would never have told the police about the books. I can't even see her going so far as to threaten to do it. That wouldn't have been at all like her."

" No, but I think she might have hinted that it would be best for Jane to know the sort of man she'd married," said Paul. " Knowing what we do now about Jane and the books, we can see the awful irony of the situation. Can't you see Roderick protesting, denying everything, begging his aunt to believe him, while she went on understandingly smiling at him? He'd have done everything he could think of, down to threatening her, all except deciding to trust Jane to believe him rather than Margot. Then would have come the surge of blind hatred and violence." Paul turned to Creed. " What's happened to Burden? " he asked. " Has he admitted the theft of the books? "

" He didn't just admit it," said Creed. " He insisted on telling us. He seemed to be determined to get it off his chest. He's gone home now, back to the barn."

Paul went on, " I don't know what Roderick actually did to Miss Dalziel. Whatever it was, it must have been over quickly and quietly, because the people downstairs seem to have heard nothing. Perhaps they were in bed already in a back room and the struggle took place in a room at the front of the house. Roderick would then have had to get rid of the body, for where it was, it pointed to him as the only possible murderer. I think he'd have left the flat noisily and obviously, gone back to his lodgings, making sure nobody heard him, then returned to the flat later very quietly. If he took his shoes off and moved about lightly, the people below, if they were still awake, would have assumed it was Miss Dalziel, getting ready for bed."

Creed grunted acquiescence. " He ran the bath-water. That would have helped to disguise any unusual noises."

" And her flat was on the ground floor, wasn't it? " said Paul. " So it would have been quite easy for him to creep out with her body in his arms. She was a small, light woman. He could have put her into his car, together with the suitcase she hadn't unpacked yet, and driven off. He'd have come straight down to the cottage, getting rid of the body somewhere on the way. And by now, of course, it'll be quite impossible to tell exactly how long she's been dead. That was important for him. He was starting to create a completely false picture of his aunt's movements, making it appear that she'd died on Saturday, because he himself could easily arrange a safe alibi for the whole of Saturday."

" Then Brian was right after all," said Rachel. " That scene in the cottage was a fake."

" Yes, up to a point he was right," said Paul, " though he jumped to the conclusion it was Miss Dalziel herself who'd faked it. In fact, it was Roderick. He must have drawn the curtains, lit the fire, taken her suitcase and coat upstairs and unpacked just enough to suggest she'd had a hasty wash on her arrival. Then he upset the coffee-table, broke the decanter and so on, and then I think he must have cut himself and let some blood drip on to the carpet."

" That's right," said Gower. " He's got a cut on his forearm—a long, clean scratch."

" There you are then," said Paul. " I think that proves what I've been saying."

The old windbag, thought Creed, remembering how much of this he had thought out for himself, how nearly he had solved the whole puzzle, he calls that a proof. He doesn't know what evidence is. He's never in his life tried to make a case to put to a jury. He hasn't got a Mrs. Meredith breathing down his neck. He hasn't got to justify his actions to his superiors. He can be as wrong as he likes and nobody's going to blame him. In those circumstances it's really quite easy to be right occasionally.

"What about the roses?" Creed asked.

"Not roses," said Paul. "Dahlias."

Creed gave his tight, uneasy smile. "The flowers in that room were roses, Mr. Hardwicke. And it happens that the purchase of them can be traced to Roderick Dalziel, but not on Friday."

"When did he buy them?" Paul asked.

"On Saturday afternoon."

"Ah yes. Naturally. But on Friday night Roderick only went out into the garden and picked some dahlias and put them in a vase. That was something, I suppose, that he knew his aunt would have done on arriving, even if she was in a hurry. And then he saw to putting the fire out, drew the curtains back again and drove back to London. He must have noticed how cold the night was growing, but it can't have been until next day that he realised how very severe the frost had become. Every dahlia in the garden here would be dead and the vase of flowers he'd left in the sitting-room would pinpoint the real time of the murder as clearly as if he'd written it up on the wall."

"Just a minute," said Dalziel. "He set that scene knowing that I was expected."

"I'm afraid so," said Paul.

Dalziel started to say something, stopped and dropped his head into his hands.

"Go on," he said.

"Well, of course he had to get rid of the dahlias," said Paul, "but he didn't dare come back on Saturday to do it. He had to be able to account for the whole of his time that day. The suspense must have been fearful. His worst danger was that Brian, who had a key to the cottage, might go in. But I imagine he knew Brian well enough to know that he didn't much care for going into the cottage. In any case, there was nothing much Roderick could do but risk its happening. He had to wait till Sunday morning."

Rachel stirred suddenly. "You mean when he went ahead with the suitcases."

"Yes. Your being at the gate made it very easy for him," said Paul. "He only had to find some reason for leaving Jane outside for a few minutes. That was all he needed. I remember seeing him from this window go off down the road with the two cases. The roses were in one of them, wrapped up, I suppose, in some damp paper, and in the cottage he simply threw the dahlias out into the dust-bin and dumped the roses into the vase they'd been in. Then he came straight out again and gave the alarm. What he didn't know was that Bernice Applin saw him throw the dahlias away and rescued them at once and came round here to sell them. When he saw them he nearly fainted. He was quite composed, after doing his telephoning to London, until he was right inside the room, where he could see the flowers, then he suddenly swayed and nearly fell."

"Yes," said Rachel, "I remember. But why did he bother with the roses? Why didn't he simply throw the dahlias away and leave it at that?"

"He'd have had to empty the vase," said Paul, "and wash it and dry it and put it away, and make sure there was no sign of where it had stood. I think changing one bunch of flowers for another was probably quicker and easier. And he had flowers and his aunt's love of flowers on his mind."

"And the Applin girl?" said Creed. "How did he find out she'd seen him dump the dahlias?"

"Jane was here when Rachel bought the flowers," said Paul. "Roderick would have questioned her afterwards about how they got here. She may not have told him that her sisters saw him too."

"She didn't know about them," said Rachel. "I told her about Bernice, but I don't think I mentioned the others."

"He killed her," said Neil Dalziel, "when he came back from doing the shopping in the village. He must have got back earlier than any of us realised and found her playing around my car in the lane."

Creed got to his feet. He remembered that only a little while ago he had thought how easily, in just those circumstances, Neil Dalziel could have killed Bernice. All the same, he had been right about Kevin Applin. From the first he had had him spotted as a murderer. Not, as it happened, in the right murder, but still his instinct had been sound. He could recognise a killer when he saw one, a real natural killer.

"It's an interesting picture you've painted, Mr. Hardwicke," he said. "It suggests a possible line of investigation. I must think it over very carefully."

Paul felt suddenly confused. There had been something else he had meant to say, but Creed's tone had put him off. Anyway, it had had nothing to do with the solution of the crime. It had been something about Bernice and her youth, about the terrible youth of all of them—Kevin, Roderick, Jane. Their youth, he had wanted to say, was the kind out of which it was impossible ever to grow up, even if they lived long enough for it, and the responsibility for that couldn't really be their own, could it? Or could it? How could one ever make up one's mind, since the results of all educational experiments were so extremely questionable. But Creed wouldn't be interested in that.

Gower had stood up with Creed. "Well, Kevin's done for himself all right," he said with an odd regret in his voice. "No doubt about that. You'd almost think he'd done it on purpose like, taking a short cut to spending his life in gaol."

"Which is what was going to happen to him anyway,"

said Creed. " Well, there are worse lives. No responsibilities, no worries, no taxes. But the crazy sort of jury you get nowadays is probably going to decide there were extenuating circumstances and send him home free as a bird to do it again and get himself hanged. It won't surprise me. Nothing surprises me." As the two men left together, he added. " Thank God I've only another two years."

>>> If you've enjoyed this book and would like to discover more great vintage crime and thriller titles, as well as the most exciting crime and thriller authors writing today, visit: >>>

The Murder Room
Where Criminal Minds Meet

themurderroom.com

9 781471 907128